# Neola

A FUTURISTIC, NAIL-BITING THRILLER
FILLED WITH ADVENTURE AND INTRIGUE

## STEVEN WEAVER

ISBN-13: 978-0-97263648-3

Published in Jamesville, New York, by The Florida Tourist, LLC - Publishing, Marketing and Advertising Agency

# Neola

A thought provoking, inspirational story that
stirs the imagination.

# ACKNOWLEDGMENTS

To my beautiful bride, thank you for encouraging me to follow my dreams.

# Preface

**The future, my present, is not what most had hoped it** would be. With technology advancing as fast as it is, one would think humankind would have made a better life for itself. Instead, morality is out the window, crime is up, and governments have taken more control.

The year is 2055. After the economic crash of the early 21st century and the collapse of the European Union that followed, the need for countries to pull together was essential. Great Britain and the United States merged to once again become people of one nation. Along with Great Britain and the United States, Germany, France, and Spain, joined in. The United Federation of States (UFS) was the result.

Large corporations have only become larger. Funding for military technology and medical advances has increased, coming from the multiple national accounts. Engineering Genetics (EnGen) is one of those corporations that has profited, moving to the top of the list of government issued contracts. By way of power, it has become above the law.

Steven Weaver

# CHAPTER 1

**Things were starting to blur. Tears and sweat filled my** eyes. I blinked to wash them clear so I could focus on her face. She was crying, but not because she was hurt. She was crying for me. She wiped tears from her face, took my hand into both of hers and said, "Hang in there, Brad. Don't leave me. You can't leave me!"

"I want to thank you for the last couple days," I said squeezing her hands. "I'm glad I got to know you."

"Don't talk like that!" she demanded. "You're not giving up!"

I smiled at her as best I could.

I could still hear the crackling fire, remnant of the explosions and small battle that had just taken place. The warehouse was ablaze, and the flickering light from the flames shined off her eyes. Outside the hangar sat the smoldering SUV and Hummer the men had arrived in, both destroyed. The SUV was on its side. Five men's lifeless bodies lay scattered around the parking lot.

Also kneeling around me was my family, all in tears as I lay dying.

"You two watch out for each other little bros," I said to

my 12-year-old twin brothers. "Always be there for the other. You are two individuals, but together you can be a force to reckon with."

"We will," they said in unison, tears running down their faces.

"Mom, Dad, I love you. Thank you for everything," I said. "Dad, sorry I always fought with you and never gave you a chance to make things up to me when you were around more."

"I understand, son," Dad said. "I didn't make it easy for you either. Just know we're proud of you. You sure have grown up quickly, becoming the great man I always knew you would."

"Thanks, Dad," I coughed, struggling to answer. Then I closed my eyes.

"We love you, honey," Mom said sobbing.

You may be wondering how I got myself into this mess. Why this strong, adventurous 17-year-old was lying here bleeding to death. Well, it started a couple of days ago. My name is Brad, and this is how my life truly began---but ended only a few days later.

# CHAPTER 2

**I was with my family: Dad, Mom, and my twin little** brothers, Zach and Parker, the day I met her. It started as a normal day, or at least our current normal.

On what was an abandoned military base-turned-makeshift city, people were scattering in every direction. Obviously something was wrong.

We watched as people spread like mice avoiding a prowling cat. Sometimes I think we felt like that too. The new joint government ensured everyone conformed. This small airfield was the site of only one band of the many groups of people around the federation, not liking the extra restrictions. Did they find us? Were they coming? It seemed as though the forces were drawing near.

Were we part of a resistance? No, we were hiding from someone worse than the government, someone who would kill you for little to no reason. A corporation that thought it had more power than the government. And maybe it did.

A car tore out from behind one of the aircraft hangars. It barreled our way, narrowly missing crowds of people scurrying away. It came straight at us. We all started to back up toward the wall, unsure of who was in the car and if they were after us. Just as the car was about 50 feet from us, the brakes locked and it slid to a stop. A mother and her daughter flew out. They ran past us through the hangar doorway. The car sat abandoned, idling directly in front of us. We all sighed with relief. Why were they in such a hurry? The mother looked terrified.

Unsure of what had just happened, or why, I looked around for answers. People seemed to be running frantically, all in the same general direction, toward us. They were running away from the north end of the base. Then I saw why. Just above one hangar appeared a massive airship. It seemed to hover under some strange new power rather than fly from propulsion as most modern aircraft did. It slowly drifted our way. Now I could see what had frightened the mother.

"Dad, look!" I hollered as I pointed to the large, silent ship floating our way. "We need to move."

"Joanne! Boys! The car. Get in!" Dad barked.

I sat in the back with my brothers. Mom and dad were in the front. Dad peeled away from the large ship, leaving behind the safety of our hangar and everything we had. We made it to the base's main entrance. The gate, which was usually open, hung closed. Guarding it were four or five government soldiers and an armored vehicle. Dad spun the car around and headed back toward the center of the base, making a right turn on the next available road. We looked for somewhere to hide, ending up near the airstrip and the hangars once again. Peering through a row of windows, I noticed the first hangar appeared to be full of small airplanes. *Why didn't we notice that before?*

"Dad, stop!" I yelled, startling everyone in the car. "There in the hangar are some airplanes. Maybe we can use one of them to get away." Dad was a pilot.

"Good idea, son," he replied and whipped into the parking lot.

We all got out and ran toward the building. The hangar looked more like an oversized crate, different from the others. I looked down at the door and then over to Dad. Someone had forced open the lock. Dad grabbed the handle and cautiously pulled it open. It creaked as we peered inside. Seemingly empty, the building was quiet. We slowly entered and closed the door behind us.

Inside, the space was huge and filled with what must have been at least 50 neatly organized small airplanes of various makes and models, all small single-propeller aircraft. Some were new and some very old. They were all strapped down to the floor, tied off as if ready for a storm. There was no sign of anyone inside.

We headed toward the ones lined up front. We crossed the hangar floor, slowed by the maze of airplane wings. The hangar seemed to go dark as if the sun had suddenly gone down. How could that be?

We continued toward the front. Nearing the first row of airplanes, I noticed Dad had separated from us. He was heading toward the left side of the hangar, likely for the door switch. He hit the large red button and with a short burst of an alarm, the door began to open. The door was about half open when all of a sudden, the building began to vibrate and shake. We all grabbed hold of the straps connecting each airplane to hooks in the hangar floor and stabilized ourselves as the vibration continued to build. It worsened until we could barely stand. A loud clunk reverberated through the metal building, as it seemed the aircraft above us came to rest on the roof. No sooner did the vibration stop we felt the building itself start to move. It shifted side to side then began to rise. The aircraft had latched onto the top of the building and started to carry it away, with us inside. We were in a shipping crate, for airplanes.

# CHAPTER 3

**The hangar we were in didn't sway back and forth as it** would have if a cable connected it to the aircraft. Instead, it was rather stable, linked to part of the massive ship.

"Now what?" I asked Dad, looking down toward the earth out the mostly open hangar door.

"I'm not sure, son," he answered, looking around the hangar. He rubbed his head in thought. What remained of the thinning hair on his head, he trimmed short. There must have been some kind of soothing power when he rubbed it because he always did that when he was trying to decide on something, or when stressed. "Since we were able to get the door open enough before the power was disconnected, maybe we can still escape in one of these airplanes. Let's check these in this front row to see if they have fuel."

"I don't like this," Mom said nervously.

I looked up. The door topped three quarters of the way open. The power must have disconnected as the aircraft attached to it, stopping operation of the door. I headed to my left as Dad went to the right. Mom and my brothers stayed where they were.

"Be careful, you two," she said. "If the hangar shifts, it

may cause you to lose your balance and fall out."

"OK, Mom," I said somewhat sarcastically. I didn't really know what I was looking for, but, I opened the doors of two airplanes as I walked around, and looked at the gauges. Yep, it's an airplane, I thought.

"Over here, everyone," Dad called after a few minutes. He motioned with his hand when we looked his way. He was standing next to one of the largest airplanes in the front row. It appeared to be an older bush cargo airplane because of the extended body and the large fat tires.

"This one is perfect," he said as he pulled his head out of the front door, "Great for landing in the terrain of the backcountry."

"Does it have gas in it? And is it safe?" Mom asked eying what was clearly a very old model. Her face revealed concern and fear.

"If it runs, it'll fly," Dad reassured her. "These were some of the most dependable airplanes in their day, and easy to fly, too. The key must be in a lock box somewhere close by. It will most likely be marked with the tail number. Let's find the key and then I can check the fuel."

"I'll go look over there, where we came in," I said and headed off while dad checked the walls closest to the airplane. Mom and my brothers stayed to unhook the airplane from the floor hooks.

I started my search at the door where we came in and moved along the back wall looking for any opening or box that might hold the keys. I reached the corner. Just on the next wall, about four feet from the floor was a gray flat steel door, flush with the wall. It seemed to me to be an electrical panel full of circuit breaker switches, and I almost walked past it at first. I decided to stop and check it out anyway. I reached up and pulled the lock lever.

"Here they are," I said in a voice that seemed to echo off all four walls. I covered my mouth as if it would take the noise back.

Dad came over and we found the key he needed. As we headed back toward the airplane, we walked by an old, post WWII-era jet. I slowed to marvel at the vintage airplane while Dad continued. What an exquisite aircraft in what must have been a fully restored condition. *I wish there was enough room in this one.*

"Dad, look at this," I said. "Wish we could take this one."

"Me, too. Looks like a replica of the original Hughes H1 jet from the 1930s. Isn't the polished aluminum beautiful?"

"Yes!"

I stood admiring the sleek surface while Dad continued to the bush airplane to ensure it had sufficient battery power and fuel. Mom and my brothers had finished un-strapping it. Dad motioned me over and just as I started around the wing of the old aircraft, the door squeaked behind me. I stopped dead in my tracks, startled by the unexpected noise.

I looked back at Dad, who motioned for everyone to get down. In walked two soldiers. They were men in their early 20s, fully dressed in the Federation uniform. Each carried a small electronic tablet and touching their screens as they entered. I was in full view of the men, if they had only looked up. I turned and looked back at my family. Dad again motioned me to get down. I made up my mind. I motioned to my dad and mouthed, "Go, get out of here."

I kept my back to the soldiers and remained standing, knowing they would eventually see me. I was going to allow them to catch me so my family could get away. Mom was going to be so upset with me, but I had to do it. Trespassers on Federation property face prison time, five years minimum! Even death if you're caught in the wrong place.

It didn't take long.

"You, how'd you get in here?" one of the soldiers asked.

Hiding my hands in front of me, so the men wouldn't see me, I waved goodbye to my family and smiled. "I love you, now go!" I mouthed. With a slight hesitation and a last look at Mom, I slowly turned and faced the men.

"Get over here," the other soldier said.

I made my way around the airplanes, strategically placed to cram in as many of them as possible. It was difficult to get around some of them, impossible around others, so I ended up crawling under the wings. Finally making it, I stood up.

"What are you doing in here?" one asked.

"How'd you get in here?" said the other before I could answer. They both stared at me.

"I came in before your ship picked this thing up," I answered as I shifted to my left, positioning myself so that if the men decided to look past me, they wouldn't be looking in the direction of my family.

"The outer doors should have been chained," one of

them said. "Did you break in?"

"No. The chain was missing and the door open when I got here. And nobody else is in here," I added in an attempt to keep them from searching the place and finding my family.

"So, you're alone?" the other asked as he looked around the hangar.

"Yes."

"Did you open the hangar door?"

"No, it was already opened."

"I'll close it," the other said as he started to move toward the switch.

I panicked, quickly looking around for something to grab or somewhere to run to distract them. Just as I decided to take off running in the opposite direction of my family, the second soldier spoke up.

"You can't close it with the switch, idiot. The power's not connected. Unless you want to close it manually, get back over here. We'll issue a work order to get someone else to come down and hook up the harness on the top of the hangar. I will enter it in." He lifted his arm and tapped a small screen attached to his wrist while the first soldier returned.

"What are you doing in here?" the first soldier continued the questioning.

"I was looking for a place to rest."

"Well, you're not allowed in here," the second soldier said. "You know there's a stiff penalty for trespassing on Federation property, don't you?"

"I do, but I became separated from my family and

they're lost."

"I think you're the one lost. You'll have to come with us."

"Where?"

"We need to take you to the captain to see what he wants to do with you. You're not supposed to be on this ship."

We turned and headed to the door. Just before we reached it, one of the men stopped and looked back. I was worried he heard something or saw them. I looked back to where my family was. I couldn't see them. The soldier turned back around and said, "I should close the door."

"Have a great workout cranking that thing down by hand," the other one said, laughing as he opened the door. We stepped through the opening. I looked back as if looking at the other man but peered past him and toward my dad. I couldn't see him or the others. The door banged closed in my face.

"It's just us going?" I asked, still concerned the other man would find my family.

"Yes."

The door led us to an elevator, sort of. The room was the end of an accordion-type corridor. With the push of a button on the wall, the corridor began to fold upon itself, raising the room upward at a slight angle. The room came to a stop and a door opened to expose a long hallway which led out of sight in both directions. As we went left, I quickly realized the other soldier had no way out of the hangar.

I tried to memorize each turn in case I was able to

separate myself from him, so I might find my way back down to the hangar. Deep down, though, I knew I was fooling myself. With a ship this size, I would never find my way back.

The soldier led me around corners and up some stairs to another level, then down long hallways and back down a few flights of stairs. We walked for what seemed like 10 minutes; all the while, we passed so many different people. We must have been on the other side of the aircraft by now.

*What was I going to do? What were they going to do to me? Would I ever see my family again? I didn't even know where Dad was going to fly if we had gotten away. Thinking back, I was stupid for letting them see me. They might have left and not found us.*

I had to do something, maybe make a break for it and try to get back to my family. But I wasn't sure what.

We rounded another corner and I found myself being led into a small corridor that had one door on the left labeled launch room and one on the right labeled storage. This was as good a plan as any. I would attempt to overpower him and drag him into the storage room.

I stopped, bent down quickly, and untied my shoelace. The man saw I had stopped and came back and stood over me as I retied it.

"Hurry up," he ordered.

"I am."

Just as I finished, I started up slowly then made a fist and launched upward catching him off guard. I landed an uppercut squarely under his chin. It drove his lower jaw and teeth directly into his upper jaw. The force was so strong, the pain so great, that he was out cold before he hit the ground. I stood there shocked by how well it had worked on a grown man. Not the first time I'd thrown the punch, but the first time on someone of his size.

I opened the storage door and dragged him in. I found some yellow caution tape they must use on the floors and wrapped his hands and feet. I finished by placing a strip over his mouth. I peeked out the door and saw the hall was still empty. Leaving him inside, I closed the door behind me and decided to see what the launch room was. I slowly opened the door a few inches and peered inside. It, too, was empty. I went in and closed the door behind me. I locked it. At first glance, it reminded me of the gym where Coach had taught me a thing or two...

# CHAPTER 4

**"Keep your hands up!" He yelled at me. "Protect your** face. You gotta protect your face!"

Blow after blow, my sparring partner took advantage of my inexperience and would pop me in the face. He would hit me in the stomach. When I would drop my hands to block another body shot, he would hit me in the face. This went on for what seemed like forever, until Coach yelled, "Stop!"

"All right, kid, take a break," Coach said to me. "Go sit down over there and I will be over in a minute."

I took my mouthguard out, my boxing gloves off and climbed out of the ring, frustrated and a little embarrassed. I sat down on the bench and looked around the room. Kids all over the gym were working out, hitting bags, and jumping ropes. There were a couple of girls in the corner lightly sparring with each other.

One kid was using the punching bag. He was good. One-handed or two, his fast rhythmic punches were consistent and timed. The bag bounced off his gloves and then the top surface with such grace and speed. I just stared in awe.

"You want to be able to do that?" Coach asked as he sat

down beside me.

"Yes," I answered, still watching the kid hitting the bag.

"Well, it's going to take a lot of hard work and determination. Do you think you have it in you?"

"I think so," I said, looking at the coach.

"You don't sound so sure."

"I want to learn to do that. It's just...I'm not sure I can do it. It all looks so hard."

"It is hard. Take Mike for example. It has taken him years to be able to hit that punching bag the way he does, years of being down here five and sometimes six days a week. Can you do that?" Coach asked looking at me seriously.

"Yes. I only have baseball after school in the spring, that's it," I said looking him in the eye for second and looking back over at Mike.

"Well, we could probably work around that," coach said and then put his hand on my shoulder. "Now tell me why you're here. Why do you want to learn to box?"

"I just like boxing," I lied to him, looking away as I said it.

"Now I know that's not the real reason," he said. "What is it?"

I sat there for a moment; his hand was still on my shoulder. He squeezed it and I looked up at him. "Because," I said then paused. "...because I want to learn to defend myself. I'm tired of guys always messing with me," I said as I looked down at the floor.

"How old are you, son?"

"Thirteen," I said.

"And how tall are you?"

"Five-foot, six-inches, but Mom said the doctor told her he thinks I will be close to six feet before I stop growing, why?"

"You're not a small kid. Don't you think they will just stop bothering you as you grow?"

"Not soon enough," I said.

"One thing I want you to know," the coach started very seriously, "I will not teach you to box just so you can use it to hurt others. I have a strict policy. If you're caught fighting, you're out! Do you understand?"

"Yes, but what if they start it? What if they push me around and knock me down?" I asked. The anger grew inside me as I thought about it.

"How many are there? Is that what they do?"

"Yes, and there are two of them. They always gang up on me and push me in my chest to try and get me to fight them." I doubled my fist in anger.

"Hey, it'll be all right." Coach said to me. "I will teach you to box, but you have to promise me you'll only use it to defend yourself. You'll never go looking to retaliate. No starting fights! Do you understand?"

"I promise."

"I mean it! Back down and walk away when they do provoke you. If I feel you're using boxing to seek revenge or hurt anyone more than necessary, I will kick you out of my gym faster than you know."

"I won't," I said. "I just want some confidence to stand up to them and make them stop."

"OK, come back tomorrow after school and we'll get

you started."

"Thank you, thank you. You won't regret it," I said, shaking his hand excessively.

"I better not!" he said. "And one more thing: I want you to start running every day. You need to build up your endurance. The mornings are the best, right when you get up. Start with short distances and slowly increase. Now get out of here. See you tomorrow," he said smiling.

"OK, thank you Coach." I turned and walked out.

# CHAPTER 5

**Inside the launch room, a small garage-type door was** opened and the blue sky exposed. The door led directly to the outside. I immediately headed toward it. My only hope was getting back to my family. Knowing they were still in the crate of airplanes and me on the other side of this huge ship, I needed to find a way to get to them. Looking out the open roll-up door, all I could see was sky.

Stepping closer to the edge, holding firm to the wall, I leaned out and could see the ground far below. To the lower right, sticking out the back appeared to be part of the aircraft's hover and propulsion system. I only guessed this because heat waves were radiating off it and trailed behind the ship. To the left, the only other visible section was about 100 yards away. The back section of it had a large opening. To its front, not connected to it, was what looked like a doorway to nowhere. Anyone walking through it would obviously fall to their death. Then it came to me. *That's where my family was.* The door was the very accordion door the soldier and I had walked through that raised and separated from the crate. It looked as though the door was still open. *If I could only get there, I thought. But how, I didn't know.*

I backed away from the door opening, which would have led to my obvious doom, and looked around. My family was in that section of the aircraft but for how long I wasn't sure. I had to get to them, and fast. I started back toward the hallway. Finding my way back was going to be impossible, but I had to try. I needed to find a change of clothes to blend in, and maybe even a weapon, or something to protect myself. I rummaged through a desk against the back wall. In the top left drawer, I found a small pocketknife, a two bladed "Old-Timer".

"Well, not the size or weapon I was hoping for, but it might work," I said and continued looking through the drawers, nothing!

I tried the lockers against the other wall, just some old clothes and tennis shoes in the first one. I moved onto the next larger locker. There was a pair of boots with funny fins on the sides and the back. *That's strange!* Hanging on the hook above the boots was a gray jumpsuit. "That's not going to help me," I said and sat down on the bench. I stared at the locker. I missed the gym back home. How I wished for a normal life again.

# CHAPTER 6

"You got this!" Coach said to me. I was sitting on the stool in my corner. My right eye was starting to swell shut. Coach held an ice pack on it as he talked. "He's worse off than you. Every time you jab with your left, he slightly drops his left hand. Fake the jab and hook with your right. If you connect the hook, then jab with your left and immediately follow with another right hook. The second time you connect, he will keep his hands up. When he does, he tends to not hold his elbows together," Coach continued. "You remember what I said about the uppercut?"

"Yes," I said. "If I connect just right, it will drive his lower jaw into his upper jaw. If his mouth is open at all, with any gap between his upper and lower jaw, the impact can knock him out."

"That's right. So after you connect the second right hook, follow it up with the uppercut. If you land it, he will go down."

"OK, Coach," I said just as the bell rang out, indicating the start of the next round. I put my mouthguard back in and stood up. Coach took the stool and climbed out of the ring. The referee motioned us to the center and said,

"Box!"

Looking at my opponent, he was probably 16 like me. He was tired, just as I was. This was the 10th round, and both of us had equally pounded the other. He was a little taller than I was. The protective headgear mostly hid his face, but his chin was exposed. I could still see his determined eyes watching my every move.

Exhausted, we both stepped toward the other and each of us threw a half-hearted punch, not really doing any damage. We then locked up, grabbing onto other. The referee came in and broke us up. He said, "Fight," and motioned us to continue.

"Jab! Jab!" Coach yelled from my corner. I stepped back in and jabbed with my right, connecting against the headgear on the side of my opponent's face. I saw him move his left hand down. I faked as if I was going to jab left but swung with my right, landing a hook to his headgear and jaw. He put his hands back up, so I jabbed with my left, hitting his gloves this time because he was protecting his face. He did it again, dropping his left hand some, exposing his right cheek. I jab left, then swung a right hook again. Sure enough, just as Coach said, the kid put his hands up to protect his face and opened his arms not keeping his elbows together.

Without hesitation, I swung my right hand up from below his chin. My glove slid between his arms and connected hard with the bottom of his chin. *A solid hit!*

I heard a click as his lower jaw closed against his upper, even with his mouthguard in. His head tilted upward as I drove through the punch. He stumbled back, hit the ropes, and bounced off. With half a twist, his body spun around then dropped to the mat. He went down hard. I looked over at the coach in amazement.

"Nice job," he yelled. "What'd I tell you?"

I looked back at my opponent, who was not moving. He was out cold.

"... eight, nine, ten," the referee counted, then stood up. He grabbed my right arm and held it up. When he let go, I jumped with excitement. My coach came into the ring and I gave him a hug. I watched as they put some smelling salt in front of the kid's nose as he lay on the mat. He jerked his head and started to push himself up but fell right back down. His coach helped him up and over to the stool in his corner.

I walked over and put my glove on his shoulder, "Nice match," I said.

"You, too," he answered, still looking dazed.

# CHAPTER 7

*I sure hope life goes back to normal soon,* I thought.

"I've gotta get out of here!" I said and stood up. I reached over and started to close the locker door. Just before it completely shut, I noticed something silver shining in the back behind the jumpsuit. I pulled the suit out. A strange-shaped helmet sat on the shelf. I took it out. It had a large, thin fin on it that extended down the center of the helmet to the back lower edge and two smaller fins on either side of it. The fins were similar to the ones on the boots. The helmet was shaped like a bullet.

I looked at the boots again, then back at the helmet. I picked up the jumpsuit. Looking closer, it too wasn't normal. There was a connecting section joining the arms with the side of the suit's body. *It looks like a flying squirrel,* I thought.

"Wait a minute!" I exclaimed aloud. "This is a flying suit. Maybe I could use it to fly down to my family and the lower section." *What was I thinking? This is crazy!* But it was my only hope. I had to try. "There's no way I could make my way back along the hallway without being seen or caught," I said aloud as if trying to convince myself. But I would only get one shot. If I missed the door, I would fly down to the Earth and away from my family, most likely forever. *Could I do it? Would it work?* I had to try.

Taking the suit, helmet and boots to the bench, I put them on. The boots were a little large for me but surprisingly comfortable. *What should I do with my shoes,* I wondered. I would want them again later. I decided to stuff them in the suit against my belly and zip it up. It, too, was a nice tight fit with extra padding in the middle, probably to make it tighter on the wearer. I put the helmet on and checked the mirror on the locker door, raising my arms out from my sides. I looked silly, but this had to work.

Nervously, I hugged the wall and inched toward the door. I stepped up to the edge with the toes of both boots overhanging and looked around. One more step and I would be falling toward Earth. *This is crazy.* I looked once again to my destination—my family's stronghold. I felt a sense of strength building up inside me as I longed for my family.

I figured I must fly straight away from the airship before making a wide turn to my left and straightening out toward the hangar's open door. If I went too far back, I might lose altitude and miss my target's opening.

The door banged. I looked back. The handle started to move. "Open the door!" A man yelled as he pounded on the door.

Deciding I couldn't waste another minute, I let go of the wall with my left hand and put my arms out away from my sides until the wing portion of the suit was tight. I said a quick, "Please God, let this work" prayer and dove away from the ledge.

I formed my best swan dive ever. *Wow, what a rush*! I was free of anything holding me back. I was flying, soaring through the air. So quiet and peaceful, I didn't want it to end. I was falling with style, and at a slow steady pace. Suddenly, fear snapped me back to the reality of my mission, as I worried about getting too far away from the ship.

I tried to look toward the open hangar door, but the force of the air on my helmet's fins wouldn't let me look too far to either side. I could see my destination below out of the corner of my eye. I felt I was far enough away to start my turn. Slowly, I rolled my body to the left and turned my head in the same direction. Surprisingly, I easily changed directions.

I continued my turn until the opening was straight ahead of me and slightly below. I looked to be on target. Then I felt myself slowing. My descent toward Earth below increased.

"Oh no!" I screamed. I was going to miss. "No!"

Now only about fifty feet away, I was level with the ledge. I didn't anticipate the turbulence and lack of air movement behind the huge crate. Inside the hangar, I could see one of my brothers sitting on the floor. My heart sank. I had let them down.

I continued to descend until my brother fell out of sight and I was looking at the lower edge of the very building I was aiming for, now 20-feet away and growing.

As I descended, a gust of air warmed my face. Ahead I

saw an identical portion of the aircraft I had seen on the other side, from my high vantage point in the upper room—the other propulsion system. Exhaust allowed me to regain speed and lift, rising on a wave of hot air.

With only about 10 feet between me and the back edge of the opening, but still lower than I needed it to be, the exhaust continued to blow me upward. Something inside me told me to arch my back, so I did. Without warning, the warm air caught my suit's wings and shot me 30 feet straight up into the air.

About 20 feet above the ledge opening, but only inches away from my destination, I straightened my body and leaned forward. I shot into the opening and instantly lost all lift, falling toward the floor. Just before I slammed into the floor, I regained my balance, straightened and landed squarely on my feet like some superhero was landing after a long flight. I bent my knees to absorb the shock, put my hand on the ground to stabilize myself, and stood up. *Wow!*

Nobody saw or heard me, luckily not even the guard who had stayed behind to close the door. I slowly took off the boots, suit and helmet and put them in the passenger seat of the nearest airplane. Then I put my shoes on. As I stood, something caught my eye. Hanging out from under the seat of the airplane, warning flags were connected to two wooden sticks. I used my pocket knife to cut off the flags and then I started to whittle a sharp point on one end of each stick.

After each stick had a nice point, I put the knife away and with a stick in each hand, I moved forward. What I was going to do with the sticks, I didn't know. The soldier who had stayed behind must've found my family because he was talking with my parents. Parker was sitting on the floor behind them with his head down. Zach was standing between Mom and Dad. I stayed low, hiding under the maze of wings spread across the hangar. I made my way around the soldier, hoping to sneak up behind him and catch him off guard.

As I closed in, Parker lifted his head. He'd spotted me! Excitement grew on his face and he started to get up as if he was going to come my way. I quickly motioned to him to stay there and to be quiet. He realized what I wanted. He sat back down and put his head into his arms. I could see him peeking at me out of his arms and smiling. I just hoped the soldier didn't look at him and realize I was there.

The soldier was yelling at my dad, something about being a spy and questioning him as to why they were there. He had Dad's hands tied behind his back, obviously his only threat, or so he must've thought. That was my advantage. Now directly behind the soldier, my mom and other brother Zach spotted me. I held my finger to my mouth in a "hushing" gesture and they both quickly looked away. I think my dad saw me as I approached, but he never looked at me directly.

Now right behind the soldier, I wasn't sure what to do. I didn't want to stab him with my makeshift weapons. The guy was just doing his job. I decided to do a sort of "chop" at the side of his neck. I'd seen it work in the movies to knock people out. Just seconds before I was to hit him, I saw Zach look. The soldier must've seen him too because he stepped to the side, and turned around as he pulled his "club" from his belt. I stared at it, relieved it wasn't a gun.

Even though we were standing at the edge of the hangar, and outside of the mix of airplanes, there wasn't much room for the fight that was about to take place.

"How did you get back here?" The soldier asked surprised. "And where is the sergeant?"

"He decided to take a nap," I said sarcastically as we circled around like two wild animals gearing up to attack one another.

"Well, I'm not going to be as nice as the Sarge; look where it got him."

"I'm sorry it has to be this way," I replied.

"You better not have hurt him, because if you did, you'll never set foot outside again."

"Your sergeant is fine, just unconscious," I said. "Just let us go and no one else has to get hurt. We were hiding from some bad people and ended up here by accident."

"Well, you're trespassing on Federation property, and as you know, that could be punishable by death."

"I can't let that happen," I said and charged toward him. Mom screamed. The soldier swung his club at my head, and I blocked it with one of the wooden sticks and then followed up with the other one, smacking him on the back of his head. I imagined it hurt. I really didn't want to use the sharpened end on him, but it looked more and more as if I needed to.

"Put those down and give up," the soldier ordered me.

"I can't do that," I answered. "Please, let us go. Nobody

needs to know we were in here. We didn't damage anything."

"Sorry, but now that the Serge is hurt, I must detain you for sure."

"OK, if that's how it is going to be," I said and charged him again. My mom screamed again, afraid for me. I held the two sticks against my forearms as protection for my arms as the soldier swung once again at me with his club. Hitting the stick in my left hand, it had no effect. I lowered my head and plowed into his gut with my shoulder, driving him into the wall. With a thud, I heard the wind expel from his lungs. He dropped the club.

"Don't let up, son!" Dad exclaimed, trying to comfort Mom as she attempted to untie him.

"Help him!" Mom yelled at Dad. "He is going to get hurt."

"He is doing fine. He's had more training than I ever had. If it starts to go bad for him, I will try something, but with my hands tied, I can't do much."

Backing away slightly, I gave the soldier the same uppercut to his jaw I did his sergeant. He took the punch much better than his superior had. After a slight pause, he came at me connecting a right hook to the side of my head. I saw stars. As they quickly faded, I saw him holding his fist that just connected with my hard head. I guessed he had broken his hand, so I drove back in and as I approached, I thought I would test to see if his hand was broken. Rather than punching his face or gut, I landed my left fist squarely on his right hand. The soldier screamed with such pain that I knew for sure he had broken it. The pain must've been too much for him because he went limp and fell to the ground.

He was out for a few seconds before he started to stir again. Before he was able to get up, I jumped on him, pulled his arms up over his back and held him down as he lay there on his stomach.

"Dad, find a rope or something to tie him up," I said as I cut the plastic tie binding his hands. I shoved an old dusty rag in the soldier's mouth. Dad handed me a roll of tape. I taped the rag in his mouth, his wrists together, and then his ankles.

"Sorry, buddy," I said to him as I dragged him to the wall and sat him up. "I'm sure someone will find you soon."

Mom stood crying, her hand over her mouth.

"Nice work, son," Dad said to me. "Sorry I couldn't help."

"Thanks, Dad. Is everyone OK?"

"Yes, we're all fine."

I walked over to Mom. She smacked me on the arm and then gave me a big hug, "Don't ever do that again!"

"I won't," I said, and looked at Dad. "Hey, if you started the airplane and dropped out the large door, would you be able to recover it and fly away?"

"If I'm able to get the engine speed up as fast as possible before we leave the doorway, and get enough air under the wings, well, maybe. The problem will be behind this hangar and the large aircraft. The air will be messed up so much that we might not be able to keep the airplane from tumbling out of control. Without air, we have no lift on the wings," Dad explained.

"Now you tell me," I joked.

"What do you mean?" He asked. "And how did you get back here anyway?"

"I flew!"

# CHAPTER 8

"I'm home," I said as I walked in the front door. I hung my boxing gloves on the coat rack and sat my bag on the floor. The midday sun entered through the windows, lighting up the living room and reflecting off the shiny hardwood floor. Our family portrait hung on the wall. Everyone looked so happy. If only that were true, things might be different. Dad was always working, never had time for me or my brothers.

Mom always kept things clean and organized. I was lucky. We had nice furniture and a big fancy house. I had a great family. Well, Mom, the twins and me anyway. Dad's home when his work doesn't need him. He's gone more than he is around. He hasn't even seen me box. Never watched any of my baseball games, nothing! I used to get so mad at him when he would come around, act as if nothing was wrong, and try to boss me. What gave him the right? Maybe if he would have spent more time at home, not worked so much, he would have a right to tell me what to do. I don't get as mad as I used to. I found a way to vent. Nowadays, my opponent in the ring feels my frustration.

Today my brothers were hyperactive, as usual. Parker was running through the living room, a game screen in his hand, Zach right behind him.

"Gimme it!" Zach yelled.

"I had it first!" Parker said, running down the hall toward the bedrooms. I just laughed.

"Boys, stop running," mom hollered from the kitchen.

I rounded the corner and headed straight for the fridge. The kitchen was as clean as the rest of the house. Everything was in its place and not a speck of dust anywhere. A nice, fancy kitchen with a large center island, it was Mom's favorite place in the house. "Hey, mom," I said.

"Hi, honey, how was boxing today?" she asked as she opened the cupboard.

"Good," I said, opening the refrigerator. I grabbed the bottle of OJ and closed the door. As I lifted it to my lips, I saw Mom holding out a glass and smiling. I took the glass from her, poured the juice into it and took a gulp. I topped it off and put the bottle back in the fridge.

"You're wearing your headgear, right?" Mom asked.

"Mom! Yes I am. I can't box without it."

"OK, I was just checking. I don't want anything to happen to that precious head of yours. So, did you talk to Zoë?" she asked me.

"Mom!"

"Well, she's cute and I hear she likes you."

"I wish you and her mom would stop trying to hook us up."

"Don't you think she's cute?" Mom said smiling.

"Yes," I said.

"Well?" she said, staring at me.

"Well what?"

"Ask her out, to the dance."

"Mom, stop!"

"What?" Mom asked.

"You know what," I said as I put the empty glass in the sink. Before I could tell her I was not ready to date and wanted to focus on my training, my brothers came running into the kitchen.

"Mom, he won't give me the screen!" Zach said.

"I had it first," Parker yelled. "I was playing and he came in and said it was his turn."

"No, you're..."

"Boys, that's enough!" She said raising her voice.

I grabbed Zach as mom grabbed Parker. "Now boys, the two of you have to learn to take turns. Now neither one of you get to play. Give me the screen," she said to Parker. "You two should go outside and play. It's a beautiful day. What are you doing in the house anyway?"

All of a sudden, the front door burst open and Dad ran in. "We gotta go," he said butting in, his voice tight.

"What's wrong?" Mom asked.

"Jack's dead," Dad said.

"What?" Mom asked.

"Your copilot?" I asked. "A crash?"

"Yes," Dad started and then shook his head. "No! I mean, yes he's dead, but no, not a crash. They killed him. We have to go. Everyone, go pack a bag. Take only what is needed: toothbrush, a change of clothes, that sort of thing."

"Wait, who would've killed him?" Mom asked,

grabbing Dad's arm as he started toward the bedroom.

"Come with me," Dad said to her. "Boys, hurry! Go pack! I mean it," Dad said looking at us.

I took the game screen from Parker. "Hey!" Parker said.

"You heard Dad. Go pack some shirts, pants, your bathroom things and a couple of things to do. Now go!" I said, pushing them out of the kitchen toward the hall as I watched Mom and Dad quietly talking as they walked. When I saw my brothers go into their bedrooms, I turned and headed straight to mom and dad's room. I stopped outside the door where I could still hear them.

"They killed him," Dad said.

"Who's they?" Mom asked.

"The company, I just know it!"

"Why would they do that?"

"Remember last week when I told you he and I had overheard something we probably shouldn't have?" Dad asked her.

"Yes, but you never said what."

"Well, his house cleaners found him and his wife dead this morning. The police said it looked like a robbery gone bad, but I know better. The other day, Jack said he thought someone was following him."

"Oh no!" Mom said.

"The police said they were killed early this morning. I came home the moment I heard. We have to go. We have to hide until I can figure out what to do."

"We have to leave everything behind? What about the boys, their school, their friends?"

"Wait a minute," I said, busting in. "You're never

around, you're always at work, and now we have to drop everything and leave because of you and this stupid job of yours. Well no, I have a life. I'm not going. You go! You're the one who overheard this conversation, not us."

"Brad, I know this is sudden and will be hard, but if I leave and you stay here, they will use you as leverage to find me and end up hurting us all anyway."

"This sucks!" I said. "Can't you just go to the police?"

"Son, you know how big this company is! I don't know how far their reach is. The police may not be safe enough. It's only for a little while, until I figure out what to do to protect us, or whom I can trust at the police or the Federation. Please, son, go pack some things now? We can talk on the road."

"OK, but you better figure something out fast. I'm not missing my senior year, or boxing for very long."

# CHAPTER 9

**Dad stopped for a moment, standing there in the** hangar. He stared at me, confused about when I told him I had flown back to the hangar.

"What did you mean?" Dad asked.

"I found this flying suit that I put on and jumped out of the upper section. I flew down here and into the hangar door just after I knocked out the other soldier," I said.

"The other soldier! Oh no! I'm sure he's awake. He'll be coming with more soldiers. We have to go!"

"Let's go. Tell me about this suit later. Come on everyone, to the airplane," Dad said to Mom and my brothers. "We're going to have to fly out of here. The soldier said trespassing on Federation property could be punishable by death. I don't want to take any chances, especially with both soldiers having been hurt."

We all headed to the airplane we had chosen earlier. Dad jumped in and turned the power on to check the system while my brothers climbed in back.

"Stay in front of that line on the floor," Dad told them. "You'll keep this thing balanced."

"You sure this'll work?" Mom asked.

"I *think* so," dad answered.

"You think so?" Mom started to drill into him.

Just as I sat back in the passenger seat, out of nowhere an old man approached my window. I screamed like a little girl. I thought he was a soldier. Realizing he wasn't, I opened the door.

"Who are you and where'd you come from?" I asked.

"My name is Michael Brandt," he answered. "My granddaughter Neola and I have been hiding here the whole time. We saw everything. Please take us with you."

"Sir, I don't know if this airplane will even hold us, let alone you and your granddaughter," Dad answered.

"Well then, at least take her," he responded as he motioned for her to come forward.

"Sir, I'm sorry..." I started to say until she came into view. Walking toward us was a beautiful girl about five feet, eight inches tall with blonde hair. She wore a floral summer dress. She was near my age, probably about 16. As she came over, I saw her eyes. They were the deepest blue eyes I'd ever seen. I couldn't take my eyes off her.

"Dad, couldn't we fit them in?" I said finally breaking free of her captivating stare, and looking over at him. "More soldiers will be coming and they'll find them, because of us."

"I see what changed your mind," Dad whispered with a smile. "OK, get in the back, both of you. Everyone must do as I say, when I say, if this is going to work. If I say get back, everyone must shift as far back past the line as possible. If I say move forward, everyone must shift to the line. Understand?"

"Yes," everyone said at once.

Just after the girl climbed in the back and the old man started in. "Stop!" yelled someone from the other side of the hangar, and a shot rang out, ricocheting off the airplane next to us. I looked back and saw the sergeant coming out of the door, and he brought a few friends with him. "Get out of that airplane!"

"Dad, we have to go now," I said as I stepped out, closed the back cargo door, and jumped back in.

"I know," he replied. 'Here we go; contact," he said as he turned the key and the engine came to life. The propeller started to spin. After a few seconds, it finally fired up in a puff of black smoke, which filled the hangar. The soldiers were coming toward us now, slowly making their way across the floor between and around the many airplanes' wings; but they were drawing near. The smoke provided a short-lived curtain between the soldiers and us.

After a few seconds, with the engine running, Dad pulled a lever out and the airplane rumbled from the power of the engine. The airplane started to move toward the opening and our possible escape.

"I need everybody to shift forward as far as you can and hold onto each other," Dad said as he looked back. "We need the weight forward to drop the nose so the tail end doesn't hit the edge of the hangar. When I say, everyone shift back as far as you can. It will be hard with the forces pulling you forward, but you must get the weight back somehow."

"Even me?" I asked.

"No, son, I need some weight up here with me." Then

Dad looked at Mom, said he loved her, and then, "Here we go."

The soldiers were only a couple of airplanes away, but we were at the edge and all I could see was open sky. It was scary. Dad had the engine at full power and airplane was starting to jump forward.

The sergeant was approaching the side of the airplane and my door. Just as he reached out for the handle, I yelled at Dad. The soldier was too late and he barely had enough time to drop flat on the ground as the horizontal stabilizer nearly hit him in the back. The airplane dropped off the edge and headed straight toward the ground. The tail end nicked the hangar's edge but the impact didn't feel hard enough to damage anything, I hoped.

Everybody screamed as we left the hangar. It felt as though we were going to fall straight to the earth and crash, but we quickly picked up speed and were instantly below the Federation aircraft.

"Quickly now, everybody to the back," Dad yelled as he pulled back on the stick, trying his hardest to raise the nose of the airplane out of its dive. The force made it almost impossible for those in the back to move. Scared, they crawled over each other until they made it to the back.

"I need your help," Dad said to me. "Grab the stick in front of you and pull back as hard as you can. We'll pull out of this, I promise."

"OK," I responded. We were moving so fast. I couldn't reach it. There was an invisible force keeping me from moving my arms. Pushing hard, I forced my arms forward. Slowly, I inched my hands closer to the stick. Finally, after giving it everything I had. I reached it.

"Everyone in the back, get ready to shift forward to the line when I say," Dad said. "Once we're out of this dive, I'm going to need the weight forward."

I pulled back on the stick. With both Dad and I pulling, we were able to get the front of the airplane to respond. Nevertheless, the tops of the trees below were coming fast.

Even though the nose was finally starting to come up, I was not sure if we would get out of this dive in time. Dad's face wasn't too reassuring.

# CHAPTER 10

**Early one evening, as usual, only me, Mom and my** brothers were home. Dad had been gone for a week now, flying some executives to D.C. They were powerful people who were lobbying for more government contracts or something like that.

We were watching a movie one of my brothers picked out. Everything was going fine, that is until he came home.

"Hey, I'm home," Dad said as he came in the front door. My brothers immediately jumped up and ran to give him a hug, racing to see who could get there first. That was something even I had done in the past, but not for a while. I used to enjoy having him come home, especially with him being gone so much. I always missed him; even up to probably a year ago, I used to get sad when he would leave because I knew he would be gone for a while. Now I just didn't care.

"Welcome home, honey," Mom said as he came into the living room. She gave him a kiss. "We missed you."

"I missed you too," Dad said. "Hi, Brad."

"Hey," I replied.

"How was your week?" he asked me.

"Fine," I said.

"And boxing?"

"Good."

"Did you have a match this week?"

"Yes, you missed another one," I said sarcastically.

"You know I would've been there if I could have."

"So you say!" I snapped at him.

"Brad!" Dad said.

"Well, what do you want me to say?" I asked.

"I just want you to understand that I want to be here, I just can't sometimes."

"I know, but it's always the same. You have to leave for days and are never around."

"I have to go where they need me to go, when they need me to go. I can't help that.'

"Yes you can! You could quit and find work somewhere else, an engineering job maybe."

"It's not that simple. Moreover, this job pays well. Enough so you can box."

"Guys, not now!" Mom interrupted. "You just got home. Can't we just be glad and enjoy each other's company?"

"You're right, I'm sorry," Dad said and sat down on the couch between Mom and me; she had just sat back down. Frustrated and angry, I got up and grabbed my car's fob from the counter.

"Where are you going, Brad?" Mom asked. "What about the movie?"

"It was dumb anyway. I ll be back later."

"Please don't go," Mom pleaded. I hesitated and looked back, thinking about staying.

"Just let him go," Dad said, not seeing that I had stopped. "I need to tell you about a conversation Jack and I overheard today that worries me. I don't think we should have heard it."

I shook my head, turned around and walked out. I got in my car. I put my finger on the sensor and started it up. I tore out of the driveway toward town. I had the car in manual mode. I hit the auto button. The car asked me my destination.

"Brandy's Drive-In," I told it.

"Calculating," the car said. "Eight minutes to your destination. I am now taking control," the car politely said to me, meaning for me to let go of the steering wheel and take my foot off the gas pedal.

As the car drove me to Brandy's, my high school hangout, I thought about how mad I get when Dad comes home and acts like nothing's wrong. I'm sure he wants to be around more and even go to my matches, but it seems he doesn't really try sometimes. I'm sure there are plenty of opportunities for someone of his experience and training. An aerospace engineer, a pilot and someone who could manage people, I know there are jobs in the city he could do and be around more, at least until me and my brothers leave the house.

Then there are those pretty flight attendants always around him and Jack. I wonder sometimes if he is messing around with one of them and is why he stays away so much. "You better not be!" I said aloud and smacked the steering wheel with my hands.

"Do you want to take over?" The car asked me.

"No!" I yelled at the woman's voice.

"OK, continuing to maintain control."

"Fine, you better!" I said as if she knew what I was saying.

After a few minutes of random thoughts of Dad flooded through my head, the car's polite, soft voice interrupted once again. "Arriving at Brandy's Drive-In, would you like me to park?"

"No, I'm taking control," I said to her sternly.

"OK, I am now releasing control," she said, and an audible alarm chimed three times at me.

I took the wheel and slowly drove into the parking lot until I found an open spot. I pulled in and shut the car off. I looked around to see who I knew. David and his girlfriend were in the car across from me. She was feeding him a French fry. *Whatever,* I thought.

"Connected," the car said to me. "What would you like to order?" The computer displayed Brandy's menu. I ordered a milkshake and authorized payment through my computer's thumbprint pad. "We'll have that right out," the computer said.

Beside David's car was an older pickup. Behind the wheel was a man in his 70s or 80s. He was sucking on a straw, drinking something. He was watching everyone. I've seen him here a lot. He either loved the food or just liked watching all the kids being young and acting dumb. The cars on both sides of me were empty, likely driven by some of the 20-plus kids over at the tables visiting. I continued to watch them outside as I waited for my shake. After a couple of minutes, a cute girl showed up with my drink. I recognized her from school. A sophomore, I think.

"Hello, here is your shake," she said and handed it to me through the window.

"Thank you," I said.

"Is there anything else?"

"No thank you."

"It's Brad, right?"

"Yes. Hi. How are you?"

"Good," she said. "Have a good night, Brad," she smiled and walked back into the restaurant. I watched her walk away until she disappeared through the door.

I sat there drinking my milkshake, or at least I tried. They were the best old-fashioned milkshakes around, so thick and creamy, so worth it. The vanilla was perfect and my favorite. I was still mad at my dad, but felt as though I was calming down some. I started thinking about how hurt I was that he was never around, but when he did come home, how he always had to take control of everything, as if Mom didn't have things in order. Mom, a little more laid back, had her gentle ways of getting us to do the things we needed to. However, she would never make me take my boxing gloves to my room when I hung them up on the coat rack at the front door where it was easier and I was less likely to forget them. I used them every day. Unlike Dad, who would usually make me take them to my room the moment he would get home. Never, "I missed you son," but more like, "I'm home. Brad, what have I told you about your gloves? They need to be in your room."

I couldn't really do anything right. Although lately, he's

not been as bad as he used to be. Tonight, he didn't say anything about my gloves. Maybe he was trying, I don't know. Stewing over my dad, I continued to watch the kids. I saw Tom, a good friend of mine. We played basketball together. I decided I would go visit with him as I finished my shake.

I got out of my car and started toward him. I went around the back of the parked cars and across the parking lot, rather than on the sidewalk. As I got close, I saw him, Joe! I slowed a little, trying to decide if I wanted to continue on or just go back to my car and leave. But it was too late. He saw me. He smiled. I couldn't go back now. It would look like I was scared.

Joe was sitting on a bench talking with a few other kids when he saw me. He stopped talking and stood up. He headed my way. *Great, here we go. I'm so not in the mood,* I thought.

"Well, look who it is," Joe said to me as he approached. He was about my height. He had bright red hair and freckles all over his face and arms. I imagined they completely covered his body by how many he had on the skin that I could see. I ignored him and stepped to the right of his path. He sidestepped to stay in front of me.

"Get out of my way, Joe. I'm not in the mood," I said to him, looking straight into his eye, now face to face. I took another step to the right.

"No!" He replied and stepped to stay in front of me. My forward momentum caused me to run into him. I put my hands up in an attempt to avoid bumping my chest into his. He must have taken that as if I were pushing him because he pushed me back.

As a reaction, I knocked his arms away from me, stopping him from pushing. Without warning, he doubled up his fists and took a swing at me. My training took over and I blocked it with my left arm and jabbed as hard as I could with my right. I landed it directly onto his nose. I felt a crunch. It hurt. I was not used to feeling that. I always had my gloves on.

He flew back and went down. He hit the ground with a thud and immediately put his hands to his nose. Blood started flowing.

"You broke my nose!" he exclaimed.

"Oh crap," I said aloud. I looked around.

"Hand me those napkins," I said to a girl sitting at one of the tables. She did. I bent down and handed them to Joe.

"I'm sorry, man, I didn't mean to," I said. "I was mad at my dad and took it out on you." Joe just sat there holding his nose and looking at me.

On the one hand, if felt good. The very person for whom I had wanted to learn to box and protect myself from was bleeding on the ground in front of me. However, I felt bad because I now knew he was all show. He never did want to fight me. He was just acting tough. Now that I was trained to box, he didn't stand a chance against me. In addition, I became a little worried that Coach would find out and kick me out of his gym.

"You all right?" I asked.

"I think so," he answered. "I don't think it's broken, just bleeding."

"That's good. Here," I said and offered him my hand. I pulled him up and we sat down on the bench.

"Man, what did your dad do to make you so mad? "Joe asked.

"Oh, he's gone a lot for work. He's a pilot and when he comes home, he immediately tries to take control of me."

"Does he hit you?"

"No, never! Just bosses me around."

"Oh, good thing he doesn't hit you. That's not fun."

"What do you mean? Does your dad hit you?"

"All the time."

"Sorry man! Is there anything I can do?"

"Will you hit him like you hit me?" Joe said then laughed. I chuckled as realized why he acted the way he did. I guess my dad really wasn't so bad.

Joe and I talked for about 20 more minutes before I decided I needed to go home and have a conversation with my dad.

"Sorry again about your nose. I really didn't mean to hit you that hard, a reaction more than anything."

"No problem," Joe said. "Remind me to never get into the ring with you." We both laughed and I nodded at him. He nodded back. I went back to my car and drove home. When I walked in the house, Dad was on his chair waiting for me.

"Son, I'm sorry I upset you," Dad said. "I don't mean to be on you all the time. I can imagine it must be frustrating for you that I'm gone so much and the moment I get home, I'm on your case about something."

"Yeah, a little," I said. "But it's not that bad. I learned

tonight there are dads that are a lot worse."

"Thank you for understanding, and I will continue to work on it. I promise. In fact, let's shake on it."

I reached out my hand and Dad took it. As he started to squeeze, I remembered.

"Ouch!" I cringed and went limp. Dad stopped squeezing.

"What happened?"

"I made a new friend tonight," I said.

"I'm confused," Dad said waiting for a more appropriate answer.

"It's nothing. Boxing wounds," I lied.

# CHAPTER 11

**I looked back at my family and our new guests. They** were all scared. I was too.

"We'll be OK, we're starting to pull up," I said to everyone. Neola looked at me and I at her. After a couple of seconds of eye contact, I smiled and returned my attention to the airplane. *She is cute,* I thought and smiled. Then reality set back in. If we didn't get this airplane under control, it didn't matter.

"Son, we need to get this up," Dad said to me a little worried. "We don't have much time."

The trees were close, and drawing nearer fast. We pulled hard on the stick. We weren't going to make it, the trees, the airplane, the trees. The airplane was slowly starting to turn up more and more with every second. Was it going to be enough?

The trees seemed so close that I felt as though I could reach out and touch them. Our nose climbed. Just as we approached the tops of the trees, the airplane leveled off. The wheels and landing gear must've clipped the trees as we started to climb, because I heard thumping below us.

"I need a couple of you to shift forward to the line to

balance the weight," Dad shouted out to them in the back. Neola and her grandfather slid forward.

We climbed up above the trees and continued back into the sky. "We made it," I said to everyone.

"Yeah," one of my brothers hollered.

"Nice work, you two," Mom said.

Dad and I looked back. Neola smiled at me bashfully. The sound of the cheers and excitement coming from the back faded and all became a blur as I looked into her eyes. "Thank you," I heard the thought enter into my head. What, did I just hear that? Her mouth didn't move. Maybe I imagined it. Imagined she said it by the way she looked at me.

"Did you hear me, Brad?" Dad asked as he touched my shoulder. "We did it, nice work."

"Thanks," I finally responded breaking my stare with her to look at him. Just then an alarm sounded. "What is it?" I asked.

"The fuel; it is low," Dad answered. "That can't be correct."

"What?"

"The fuel is out. It was full when we left, I checked."

"What could have happened?" I asked him. "Could it have been wrong before?"

"Possibly, but in all likelihood we damaged something when we hit the treetops," he answered. "Maybe a branch punctured the fuel tank."

"What do we do?" I asked.

"We need to find a place to land, and fast," he responded.

"It's all trees below. There's nowhere."

"Wait; is that a clearing over there?" Dad asked.

"It might be," I answered as he banked to the left toward the spot.

We were descending in preparation for landing. "What is that, a fence?" I asked pointing to the trees.

"It looks like a large electrical fence," said a voice between Dad and me. We both looked back to see the old man on his knees between us.

"Why would an electrical fence of that size be out here in the middle of the woods?" my dad asked almost rhetorically. As we flew over the fence, we saw a sign that read, "EnGen, Private Property."

"EnGen? What?" I asked. "Out here?"

"I don't know, but they have many subsidiaries, divisions, studying all sorts of things," Dad answered. "I wish we had time to find another place. That's all we need, to be on their property."

"They call that their animal sanctuary," the old man said. "We don't want to land in there; we mustn't!"

All the while, the beeping of the low fuel warning continued. We must've been running on fumes by now.

"Well, I'd try to turn around but the fuel markers are on empty and when we were higher, the clearing up ahead was the only visible place for a safe landing," Dad said as he silenced the alarm. "Why don't we want to land inside the sanctuary?"

Before he could answer dad's question, the engine stopped. A new set of alarms and beeping began, only this time more rapidly.

"What happened," Mom asked in a panic when the airplane went silent. "Did the engine just shut off?"

"Yes, honey, so everyone hold on to something," Dad said. "Well, it looks like it is the clearing now, no matter what. We should be able to glide to the clearing safely, but the landing might be rough," Dad continued with his best attempt to reassure everyone.

"Mom, are we going to die?" Parker asked.

"Yeah, how do we fly without the engine?" Zach added.

"No, Parker, we're going to be OK. Dad can fly this thing without the engine. He is going to land it in the field down there. Just hold tight onto me," Mom told them, but the look on her face when she finished said she was not sure she believed it herself.

The airplane slowly descended, and the treetops once again became an issue. The clearing was near, and seemed to grow the closer we got to it, as did the tops of the trees. We cleared the trees and were over the open field, drawing close to the ground. Dad did well to keep the airplane level as we slowed.

The clearing looked smooth enough. I remember the tires on this airplane looked larger than normal and probably had been designed to land in fields just like this.

We were only a few feet off the ground. Everyone held onto the walls, seats, and cargo straps—anything they could to brace for the initial impact between the tires and the unknown terrain below. We were still coming in fast. We were approaching the clearing midway through it, and the forest of trees ahead was coming close.

Without warning, the tires made contact with the

ground and bounced off the grassy field, launching us back a few feet into the air. Then with less force, we hit the ground again. This time we didn't bounce so hard. With one last small hop, the tires maintained contact with the ground. Now we were heading out of control across the field and toward the trees, fast. Dad was pushing hard on the pedals. The flaps didn't seem to slow us very fast.

"Will we stop in time?" I asked.

"It's going to be close," Dad answered. "Help me by pushing both of those pedals at the same time."

"OK."

The trees ahead of us were coming closer fast. We were slowing, but it appeared not fast enough. The trees were only a few hundred feet ahead, and we headed straight toward the trunk of a large one.

"Son, take your feet off the brake for a second," Dad instructed.

"Why?" I asked as I released them.

"We're heading straight toward that tree. I want to try to steer beside it so the wing hits it instead of the prop."

Dad let off the brakes and pulled the control stick to the side, and the airplane turned as it bounced along the field.

"Now!" He yelled at me and we both pressed once again on the pedals. We began to slow, but it still wasn't going to be enough.

"Hold on!" I yelled to everyone as I saw the trees approaching quickly. There was a huge jolt and a loud crack. I was thrown forward, held in place by the seatbelts. I stopped short of the windshield. I could feel someone hitting the back of my seat. With nothing to stop him, the old man flew between the front seats and into the control panel. As fast as it started, it was over.

# CHAPTER 12

**I shoved a couple pairs of pants, five or six shirts,** and other clothes I felt I needed into my bag. I ran into the bathroom and grabbed everything from floss to my shaver. I took what I felt I had to have for a week or so, as I was sure we were only going to be away for that long. *It had better not be longer!* I thought.

"If you're done, we need to load the camping gear. We're going to hide out in one of our camping spots." Dad said to me stepping into the bathroom.

"Where?" I asked.

"I'll tell you on the way. I don't want to chance it if someone is listening somehow," Dad said looking around as if trying to spot a microphone or hidden camera.

"OK," I said, somewhat chuckling at his apparent paranoia.

"Joanne, we're going out in the garage," Dad said. "Will you pack as much food as you can?"

"Yes, but I don't like this," mom said. "I'm worried. Do you really think they would do something to you, or to all of us?"

"I don't know, honey, and I don't want to chance it, at

least until I can figure something out."

"OK, but how are you going to figure out their intentions?"

"I don't know that yet either."

Dad and I went into the garage. We stacked sleeping bags, tents, a stove, chairs and a small table, as well as anything else we thought we would need, into the back of the truck. I checked the battery charge. "It's full," I called out to Dad.

"Good, go ahead and unplug it," he said. "Let's go get everybody's bags and load them up. I want to head out in a few minutes."

"OK," I said, still a little frustrated about leaving. I understood why, but wished we didn't have to. We ran back into the house, grabbed the bags of food as well as the icebox with the eggs, juice and everything else cold from the fridge and took them out to the truck. Back and forth we went until everything was loaded.

"Boys, let's go," Dad called down the hall to my brothers. They came out of the rooms.

"Do we have to go?" Parker whined.

"Yeah, I want to stay," Zach added. "I want to play our new game."

"Later!" Dad said impatiently. "Get in the truck."

After we all climbed in the truck, dad opened the garage door and pulled out. Leaving the driveway, Mom looked back at our house as the garage door closed. "Why do I get the feeling we won't be back here again?" she asked rhetorically to Dad in a low voice so my brothers and I wouldn't hear. I don't know about them, but I heard her.

Dad put his hand on her arm to comfort her but didn't say a word.

We drove for about an hour, toward Tillamook. Drizzling outside, the rain appeared to be stopping. I could see the clouds were breaking up. I didn't want to set up camp in the rain; that always sucked.

We were only a couple of miles away from our turn off the main road, when Dad noticed them. "I think there's a car following us," he said.

"Oh, John," Mom said to Dad as she turned and looked out the back window. I, too, looked back. A silver sports car was about 50 yards behind us.

"How do you know?" I asked Dad.

"I was not sure at first, but the more I thought about it, the more I realized the car had been back there for at least 45 minutes. I blew it off at first thinking I was being too paranoid, but later realized it looks like one of the EnGen's corporate cars."

"What are we going to do?" Mom asked.

"Let's see them follow us now," he said and hit the brakes. He turned right, sliding onto a Forest Service road. We all looked back in anticipation. Was the car truly following us? Would it turn or continue down the highway?

"There it is," I said. "It's turning. They're following us."

"I have a plan," Dad said. "Remember when we were camping up here three years ago and we got stuck on that washed out dirt road?"

"Yes," Mom and I answered.

"I'm going to lose them on that road. It's up here a little

ways."

"What if it is too bad and we get stuck?" Mom asked. "It would make it easier for them to catch us. All the way up here, in the middle of nowhere, we would surely be killed."

"We won't. I will make a run for it in four-wheel-drive and not stop. Before, when we got stuck, we were driving slow and I didn't know what to expect. This time, I'm prepared."

"I hope you're right," she said. The car sped up and was getting closer. I think whoever was driving it knew that we knew they were following us and realized it didn't matter anymore. "They're gaining on us," I said. "How much farther?"

"It's just up here. I can see the road."

"Good. Hurry," Mom said, watching the car behind us.

"Hold on," Dad said as he slid around the corner. My brothers were laughing and having fun, but the rest of us knew how serious this was. The car slid around the corner in pursuit.

The road was smooth and in great shape. I wondered if we took the right one, or they had fixed it. It was three years ago when we were here last. Just as I was about to ask Dad that very question, he rounded a small curve in the road and said, "Here we go! Hold onto something." Just ahead was a section of the road that had a 50-foot-long mud puddle on both sides, where each tire would ride. The water hid their true depth.

"What if they're too deep for us and we bottom out?" I asked too late. We were already into them. A splash of water flew into the air as the front tires hit the puddles.

There was a loud bang as our front bumper crashed into the dirt separating the two rows of water. We all flew forward. Good thing we were all in our seatbelts.

Dad had to turn the wipers on high because so much dirty water splashed up on the windshield and instantly blocked our view. Dad drove through it. There was a loud clanking noise that made its way front to back, along the underside of our truck.

"What was that?" I asked Dad.

"I think it was the plastic part of the front bumper," he answered.

We didn't stop, but hitting the dirt and running over the bumper did slow our progress some. Dad stomped on the gas and continued forward. Water was flying out in all directions. We were going so fast I wondered if there was even going to be any water left in the ruts.

I look back for the car, and through the flood of water, I spotted it. The car was sliding sideways in an attempt to stop before hitting the mud puddle. It couldn't go around them because trees were too close and thick on both sides of the road.

The car was too light, and with the slick mud there was just no way for it to stop. It slid out of control and into the ruts. The left side of the car went directly to the bottom of one. When it did stop, it came to rest with the driver-side tires suspended a few feet in the air. High centered, the sportscar was stuck. Steam blew upwards as the water flooded onto the electric motor. He was not going anywhere anytime soon.

We splashed though the puddle and continued until we

came to the next forest service road. We turned left and headed back to Highway 26.

"Where we going?" Mom asked.

"Back toward Portland, I guess," Dad said, a little unsure. "We can't camp here now because they would eventually find us. They have to come up and get that car out of the mud, and more of them will show up, and likely scour the area for us."

"So now what?" I asked.

"I don't know," he said.

We were all scared now. Dad was right. They were after him. We had to disappear somehow. *But how? For how long?* I wondered. *So much for boxing and enjoying my senior year,* I fumed. I wanted to scream at Dad. It was all his fault.

That job of his has been hurting this family for years, and now this! My fear had quickly turned to anger. I had to calm myself down or I was going to blow up. That wasn't going to help anyone. I decided to think about something else. I wasn't going to let this make me somebody I didn't want to be. I didn't like being angry with Dad all the time. I didn't like hating him. I was lucky to have both my parents in my life, and together for that matter. So rare!

I sat back in the seat, between my brothers. I watch them play on their handheld screens, hoping they didn't get angry and begin to hate Dad as I had. Then I thought about high school, about what was to happen after I graduated. Well, now that this has happened, I didn't know what I would do. I didn't even know if I would be able to finish high school this year. That would suck! Having to finish next year and not graduating with my friends, all because of Dad and his job. I started to get angry again. It seemed everything that was going wrong in my life lately pointed back to him.

I shifted my mind from Dad. Maybe I will try to box after high school, professionally. That would be fun. It could pay well, but I really didn't want to get beaten up for a living.

We drove for what seemed like an hour, but I lost all track of time. I knew we were close to Portland because of the scenery. All of a sudden, an alarm went off. "Oh no," Dad said.

"What is it?" Mom asked a little panicked.

"Our battery is low," he said. "It shouldn't be. Maybe it has something to do with the mudpuddle. Maybe water or mud ended up somewhere it shouldn't have and caused the battery to drain faster. On the other hand, it could've just been from powering through the water and the mud. Either way, we have fifteen minutes to find a place to stop."

"I have no idea where." Mom said. "I haven't been on this side of town much." She looked out her window for ideas. She was quiet, staring.

"Honey," Dad said to her, "pull up the map and let's zoom out and see if we can find a place."

"OK," she said and touched the truck's computer screen. I leaned forward so I could also see it. She pulled up the map showing our current location, heading southeast on Highway 26. Initial scans of the map weren't producing any ideas.

"I know! Here," Dad said and pointed to an area on the screen. As he pointed, he put the car in auto drive. "Zoom in there."

Mom did. There was an old military base displayed on the map. "Why there?" I asked.

"That base was built back around 2025. It closed when the Federation states began to take over. There are some old aircraft hangars there where people who do not have a home currently live. But..." he faded off.

"But what?" Mom asked.

"But it is said to be the area where some of the last groups of resistance hang out. But those are only rumors. It is our only hope right now."

Neither of us argued with him. We had to go somewhere. If a group of resistance were there, there's a chance Federation military would raid the place, but they also could've already done so.

Dad made a couple of turns and headed toward the old base. The low-battery alarm went off every few minutes. We only had five minutes of battery life left when we reached the entrance.

The red metal gate that should've been across the road blocking the entrance stood open. A large sign read, "No Trespassing on Federation Property" hung off one of the posts. We entered anyway.

Abandoned buildings were everywhere. They became larger and larger as we headed toward the runway where the hangars were. More and more people were around as we drove on. People walked in all directions. Others had set up tents and were sitting out beside them.

"There," Dad said, pointing to the row of large hangars. "Let's see if we can find room in one of those. We will at least be out of the weather."

"Warning, low battery," the car's alarm spoke. "Immediately find a safe place to pull over."

"Well, it looks like we will start here," Dad said as he stopped next to the first hangar we came to. He shut the power off and turned in his seat to look back at my brothers and me. "Brad, I want you to stay here with your mom and brothers. I need you to watch our stuff while I look around."

"OK," I said.

"Be careful, and hurry back," Mom told him and gave him a quick kiss on the lips.

"I will."

Dad was gone for about 10 minutes. He found a place inside the first hangar. We unloaded our stuff and set up the tent, tables and other belongings inside a back corner of the hangar. No other space was available. Camping indoors, that was new.

After we were finished setting up, I stepped away from the tent and stood there looking around. There were many other families just like us with their tents and boxes of stuff. Everyone looked sad, as if they'd lost all hope. I didn't want our family to end up that way. We just couldn't. We had to figure something out and fast.

# CHAPTER 13

**There was silence for a few seconds after we crash-**landed, before everybody started to stir. I think everyone was surprised we made it. I pushed myself away from the dash and sat up. The windshield was shattered. A branch was only a few inches away from my dad's face; it just missed him. I shook my head to remove small particles of glass from my hair. I shouldn't have done that because instantly my head started to pound. In the back, everyone was piled into a heap behind the seats, but they all seem to be OK.

"Is everyone all right?" Dad asked, looking at everyone piled on each other.

"We're OK back here," mom answered.

"I think I'm OK, but my head hurts," I said.

"How about you?" Dad asked the old man as he helped him back to his knees. "Are you all right?"

"I'm OK. Just bruised, I think," he answered. "And please, call me Michael."

"All right Michael. It looks like you have a small cut over your right eye. Here, take this," and he handed him his clean handkerchief.

"That was nice flying and probably the best emergency

landing I have seen," Michael said. "You saved our lives."

"Thank you. I did the best I could. I had a great copilot," Dad said looking at me. He put his hand behind my neck and squeezed slightly as he smiled. I pulled my shoulder away and thought, *"Now he wants to show me appreciation and affection?"*

"Let's gather everything we can find. Look in all the compartments, under the seat and everywhere else supplies could have been stored," Dad instructed everyone as he opened his door to climb out, taking one last long look at me.

Everyone collected what we could and we all got out of the airplane. Mom took the first-aid kit and tended to Michael's wound. Thankfully, no one else was hurt.

"What do we do now?' I asked Dad looking back at the remains of what used to be an airplane. The right wing was missing and the left was severely damaged, impact from multiple trees.

"Let's rest for a few minutes and then look at everything we found," Dad said. "It's going to be dark soon, so we'll have to sleep here tonight and figure out something for the morning."

After Mom finished cleaning and bandaging the cut above Michael's eye, he came over to Dad saying he needed to talk to him about something.

"Sure, what's on your mind?"

"Can we talk in private?"

"OK, but is it something Brad can hear? He is my second in command if something happens to me," Dad said smiling at me. I just rolled my eyes.

"That's fine."

"Let's step over here then," Dad said.

The three of us moved away from everyone to have a discussion. Michael seemed worried about something. His demeanor was as if someone was coming, because he kept looking around the woods.

"All right, what's up?" Dad asked.

"As I started to say on the airplane before we ran out of gas, I don't think it is going to be safe here within EnGen's fence," Michael said.

"I agree that I don't trust EnGen, but why? What do you know about this place?" Dad asked. "I used to be a pilot for EnGen but I never heard about it."

"It's a strange coincidence, but I too worked for EnGen. Later, when we have more time, I'll tell you more about my job there, but for now just know I was a scientist. This is what we call The Sanctuary—not to protect the animals from man, but rather to protect man from the animals."

"What do you mean?" I asked.

"A division of EnGen is testing DNA alterations on animals," he started. "In other words, they would take the DNA genome from a specific animal, alter it, and grow it from an embryo to see if what they thought they were altering would actually change. They were successful altering some aspects but didn't know what else it altered, if anything. They would raise the animal in the lab and let it out into the sanctuary for observation. They wanted to see what would happen if the animal continued to grow to maturity. They also let test animals breed naturally with unaltered animals of the same species to see if the offspring would be affected."

"That's crazy! What makes them think they can play God like that," Dad said.

"They're still conducting the studies. I wasn't part of that division but can only imagine what they were doing," Michael continued.

"So were some of these test animals dangerous even before messing with them, or were they squirrels and other small animals like that?" I asked only hoping.

"I don't know, but I assume they played with the dangerous, more intelligent animals. That's why I felt it wasn't safe inside the fence," he answered. "Do you have any weapons?"

"No. It never seemed necessary. We're trying to hide, blend in, not create a manhunt by shooting someone," Dad said. He was lying. He did have a gun with a few bullets, but he never liked to use it, or show it. He especially didn't want to shoot someone just because we'd crash-landed inside their fence.

"So what now?" I asked.

"We need to find a way out of here as soon as possible," Michael answered.

"Son, I need you to find some sturdy, heavy sticks. Then use your knife to make long spears, one for everyone in the group. Also, make a few shorter forearm-length spears like those you did before. Make them as fast as you can. I will get a fire started. Michael, here, take my knife, go back to the airplane, cut open the seats, and take out the foam padding. Bring it, along with the seatbelts. We can cut the belts in strips and tie the foam to the long spears to light on fire. This may help keep any dangerous animal at bay."

We all went our separate ways. Dad set up the fire near the airplane to allow Mom, Neola and my brothers access to its cabin for a safer place to sleep. I completed my spears and Michael tied his foam to the ends of them. He then took a screwdriver he found and, using a rock, punctured the airplane's oil pan. Holding the foam under the stream of oil, he rotated it to allow the oil to saturate.

"The oil will make our spears easier to light and stay lit longer," he told me.

As evening set in, the shadows from the trees grew longer. Knowing what Michael had told us, I wasn't looking forward to the sun disappearing behind the horizon. Dad had a nice fire going and it made me feel better, but only a little. The noise from the crash would likely draw curious animals in.

We were all sitting around the fire making small talk while Mom gave everyone granola bars and a drink from the water bottles she had. Mom didn't say how she felt much, but we could see it on her face and in her actions. When worried, she would always baby my brothers and me. That was how she was acting.

"Mom, you OK?" I asked her.

"Yes, Brad. I'm OK," she said with a smile. "This day has been a roller coaster of emotions for me. I will be better in the morning when we can get moving again and get out of here."

"I love you, Mom," I said.

"I love you more," she replied. We'd played this game since I first began to talk, but under these circumstances it didn't feel right to have fun.

As the sun set, the night air cooled fast. Fortunately for us it was August, so we didn't expect it to get too cold, even up here in the Oregon forest. But the fire felt nice.

Neola was sitting across from me, and I had a hard time not staring at her. The flickering light danced in the reflection of her eyes. She looked up and smiled at me. Parker was sitting next to her enjoying the fire. I decided to move closer to her to talk to her. I got up and walked around the fire. I bent down, grabbed Parker from behind, picked him up, and swung him back-and-forth. He was probably a little old for that now, but I kind of used it as an excuse to trade places with him. I knew he would want me to let go and move somewhere else around the fire.

"You did great Parker, on the ship I mean. I know you saw me, but to stay there and act like you didn't, nice job!"

"I knew you were trying to surprise him," he said as he squirmed to get out of my grip. I held him a little longer than he'd like and gave him a big squeezing hug. He got embarrassed with Neola sitting there watching. Breaking free from my hug, he pushed himself off and went over to the empty spot where I had been, next to Zach.

"He's a good kid," I said to Neola. "They both are."

"They seem to be," she said.

"Do you have any brothers or sisters?"

"No, it's just me."

"Well, they're fun. I think it works because they're so much younger than me."

"It does seem like they really look up to you. You have a nice family."

"Thank you. We have our issues, like any other family. Overall, they're great. What about yours? Where are your parents? If you don't mind me asking?"

"I never knew my parents. Michael, I mean Grandfather, is all I have."

"Oh, I'm sorry," I said feeling guilty.

"That's OK. It's not your fault. You didn't know."

"So, hope you don't mind me asking another question; what forced you and your grandfather into hiding? Is it the same as us? EnGen?"

"Yeah," she answered hiding her eyes as if uncomfortable looking directly at me saying it. "Michael is protecting me, us from those who may want to harm us." Neola got a strange look on her face and cocked her head a little.

"What is it?" I asked.

"Did you hear that?" Neola asked.

"Hear what?"

"It's like someone talking."

"I didn't hear anything," I responded. "Just Dad and Michael."

"I don't think so. It was different."

"Like what?" But before I could ask...

"There it is again!" She interrupted me. "Did you hear it now?"

"No." I answered as I stood to my feet. "Dad, can you come over here," I whispered as I motioned him over.

"What is it?" Dad asked as he and Michael came over.

"Neola said she is hearing voices out there," I answered.

"Is that true?" Michael asked her.

"Yes, it sounds strange, though."

"Is it something you're hearing with your ears, or something with your mind?" He asked her. Looking over at me and Dad, he said, "I will explain later."

That was a strange question. *What did he mean, with her mind?* I wondered. *Who could hear things with their mind? Who were these two, and what were they not telling us?*

"My mind, I think," she said. "But it is still hard to tell the difference."

"Close your eyes and concentrate like I taught you," Michael instructed. "Try to pick out the thoughts you heard earlier. Just picture you're looking through a lens and then zoom in on the specific voice from a few moments ago."

"I'll try," she said and closed her eyes.

"Good. Now breathe slowly. Relax," he said gently. "Do you see where to focus?"

"Yes," she answered.

"Good, you're doing fine," Michael encouraged her. "Now zoom in and pick out the words from the voice."

Dad and I were just staring at the two of them, unsure of what we were even seeing. By this time, Mom was finished with the makeshift bedroom inside the wrecked airplane. My brothers, who were under the only blanket we had, were giggling at each other.

"What's going on?" Mom whispered to Dad as she walked up to us.

"I'm not sure," he whispered back as he slowly raised his finger with a gentle gesture to get her to stop talking so he could hear Michael and Neola. Mom turned toward Michael to listen.

"OK, got it," Neola said. "It is a strange language."

"Translate to English; you can do it," Michael said.

Neola began to translate, "You two go around that way, and I will stay here until you're in position. Then we will move in together, slowly."

"They're close and surrounding us right now," Neola continued as she somewhat came out of her deep focus.

"Brad, get the spears ready to light," Michael ordered. "We're going to need them."

"Yes, sir," I answered and went to the front of the airplane and collected all 15 of them. I brought them back and handed three to everyone.

"Stay in the airplane no matter what happens," Dad said to my brothers as he closed the back door. "Only light one torch at a time. We need the fire on the spears to last as long as possible."

My brothers knelt in front of the side window of the airplane to get a better view of the commotion outside. They were still giggling and poking at each other, unaware of the approaching danger.

"What if they have guns?" I asked.

"Then these spears won't really help us," Dad answered.

"Anything else, Neola?" Michael asked her.

"No, but they're getting closer," she answered. "I can feel them."

The adrenaline was pumping through my body. My hands were starting to shake from the suspense of not knowing who was out there or what they might do to us for being on their property.

"They're here!" Neola screamed, snapping me out of my thought.

# CHAPTER 14

**I looked around but couldn't see anything. "Where?" I** asked, seeing nothing but pitch black.

"One right there, and the other two are over there and there," Neola answered pointing into the darkness of the forest as if she could see them and expected us to as well.

"I don't see them," I answered, but then something near the ground caught my attention. I didn't see them at first because I was looking up, for men walking. A pair green eyes faintly reflecting the light from the fire. *Were they crawling? Why were their eyes glowing so greenish orange? Night vision?*

"Look down, on the ground! I think they're crawling," I said, assuming the others were also looking up. That was when everyone began to see them.

"Light your first torch," Dad ordered. "Be ready."

"Who are you?" Michael called out. "We mean you no harm. We crashed our airplane and are waiting until daylight to get out."

"Show yourselves!" Dad yelled after no response to Michael's plea. After a few moments, still nothing.

The eyes watched us, but they did not move forward.

They stayed just out of the radius of the fire's lights, as if calculating a strategic attack, waiting for the right moment.

All of a sudden, the eyes moved forward. Rather than a man coming out of the darkness, what stepped toward us was completely unexpected—a large black cat. Its eyes had human-like qualities, yet obviously were not human. A black panther? Well, sort of.

Mom gasped as she looked at Dad then me, and then back at the twins in the airplane.

The cat slinked forward, stepping farther into the light, revealing itself. The cat was not normal, like a black panther. It didn't have the fur one would expect. It had more of an alligator skin, rough and scaly like body armor.

"What is it?" I asked.

"It looks like one of their experiments," Michael answered. "Don't underestimate its intelligence."

"And Neola heard and understood its, thoughts?" I asked. "How?"

"I will explain later," Michael answered. "We need to focus on working together to get out of this."

"How are these little wooden sticks I made going to get through that thick skin?"

"Neola, try to talk to it," Michael said, ignoring my question. "Use your thoughts. See if you can convince them to leave us alone."

"OK, I will try," she said staring, at the one directly in front of her, likely the dominant of the three. All the while, the other two were inching closer.

"It won't listen to me," Neola screamed. "He wants the

two boys, and if we give them to him, they will leave the rest of us alone—for tonight."

"But tell him they can't have them!" Dad said.

"Hell, no!" I added. Mom started crying.

Neola spun and looked back at the aircraft. "There's another one, there!" She said pointing.

My brothers started to scream. We all looked back to see a fourth cat using its claws to open the side door. It had just pulled the latch when I threw my flaming stick while Mom was yelling at it to get it to look away.

My spear struck the side of the cat's large head. Sparks erupted in a bright flash causing the cat to back away as the spear bounced onto the ground and the flames flared up. The armored cat turned toward me. I put my second stick into the fire. It lit as the predator stocked forward. The cat took two steps and lunged, launching an easy six feet into the air, directly over the fire and right toward me. I backpedalled to escape.

All of a sudden, a voice inside my head said to stop and step forward, toward the cat. The voice was strong and commanding. Without question, I did as it said. Now that I was directly underneath it, the cat's stomach looked to be covered with the same impenetrable skin.

Just below the rib cage, the voice said. I saw a section in the armor, now lit up by the fire, that exposed bare skin.

With only a split second to react, I took my spear in both hands. As the cat came down on me, I drove the red-hot stick directly into the only vulnerable spot I saw on the beast. It let out a scream I never want to hear again. The spear entered the cat's chest with little effort. Its own weight came down on the stick, which by now was wedged against the ground. My hands slid down to the end of the stick that disappeared into the cat. Half the cat's body, which must have weighed a couple hundred pounds, came down on me as the rest larded hard on the ground.

Immediately upon impact, the cat howled once more and then started to spin and buck around. It flipped and jumped, making its way back into the forest and out of sight. We could hear the cat's cries fade as it ran farther and farther away.

My left hand started to throb. Looking down I realized I must have grabbed the section of the stick that was on fire because my palm was red with black char around it. But I didn't have time to think about that right now.

Meanwhile, the other three cats drew closer, held back only by everyone whipping and waving their flaming sticks. Neola was becoming angry with them.

Then, as if not afraid of the sticks and fire any longer, all three advanced with two giant leaps forward. They were right upon us and ready to attack. We all prepared ourselves. *Was this the end?* What a way to go.

Just then, a scream resonated from Neola so loud it stopped the cats in their tracks and scared all of us. "STOP!" She demanded. "Get out of here and leave us alone!"

The three suddenly turned away from us and casually started to walk off, as if nothing had happened.

"Neola," Michael said, "tell them to stop."

"Why?" Mom asked. "They're leaving; don't try to stop them now."

"Just do it, Neola," he continued as he held his finger in the air toward Mom, motioning her to wait one moment. Mom stood there staring at him as if to say, "You didn't just hush me!"

"Stop!" Neola ordered, and the cats responded.

"Tell him to turn around."

"Why?" I demanded.

"Turn around," Neola said to the cats, ignoring me.

"Now tell him to lie down," Michael said.

"Lie down!" Neola ordered, and without hesitation, all three circled once, tucked their paws under their chests and lay down.

"Do you know what is happening, honey?" Michael asked Neola.

"No, what?" she asked. "Why are they listening to me now?"

"This is exciting," he said. "You're controlling their minds."

"You mean I can make then do what I want?"

"Yes. We were hoping you had this in you. It took fear, anger and the stress of the situation to bring it out. You were worried about the safety of the people around you and decided enough was enough, I guess."

"You! Stand up!" Neola ordered to the dominant cat in the middle. It stood. "Lie down, now!" It obeyed. "Get up, and go climb that tree," she said to the cat and pointed to the nearest tree. It stood, turned and headed directly to the tree. When it approached, it leapt nearly 10 feet up the tree and started to climb it. "Stop and get back down here!" She demanded. It did and made its way back to the other two still lying on the ground. "Lie down!" It did.

"Neola, I have an idea," Dad said. "Maybe we can use these three to surround us and keep watch over our camp until morning. We have no idea what else is out there, and these three would make great allies."

"Are you crazy?" Mom yelled.

"Actually, it's a good idea," Michael chimed in. "We have studied mind control, and Neola should maintain control, even when she sleeps. She can't release them until she is ready to and forces the disconnection. But even if she just told them what to do, they'd think it was their idea anyway and maintain it until she told them something different."

"I don't know if I would feel safer with them near, watching over us, or far away and not knowing if they would come back," Mom said.

"I know what you mean," I added.

"I will do it," Neola finally said. She stared at the three cats and after about 30 seconds, they stood up and all three went off in different directions. "There, I told them to circle the camp all night and not let anything or anyone past. I also told them I didn't want to hear or see them the rest of the night. At dawn they're to check in with me."

"You think they understood that as a human would?" I asked.

"They should," Michael answered. "They're very intelligent and have probably been altered with human DNA. Neola can have conversations with them as if talking to one of us."

"So, this might be a good time for that explanation you

promised us earlier," Dad said. "Who are you two, and how can she do these things?"

# CHAPTER 15

**Michael, Dad and I all sat down by the fire.** Mom and Neola moved into the aircraft to be with my brothers, as well as to try to calm down and maybe get some rest. Since it was late, we were all tired, but none of us felt we were going to be able to sleep.

"So what is this all about?" Dad asked Michael.

"Neola is not my granddaughter," he began. "But first, let me say I'm glad we ran into you and your family. I was so worried about what we were going to do. I'm way over my head here. I have no idea on how to hide or disappear so people can't find us.

"OK, so let me go back about twenty years. I worked for a small medical division of EnGen. We were working to map the neurons of the brain. We felt if we could map a healthy person's brain and compare that to a diseased brain, then we might be able to see what may be going wrong, or missing."

"How would you be able to map the brain?" I asked. "In our science class, we learned there are billions of neurons."

"One hundred billion, actually," Michael corrected me. "These neurons couldn't be tracked or followed, until later discoveries showed that water followed the complex structure arbors."

Dad and I must've had blank stares, because Michael said, "Sorry, arbors are bridges. They connect the pathways. You see, with water being a major part of our makeup, it is only reasonable to believe water would follow and moisten these bridges."

"Oh yeah, obviously!" Dad said and we all laughed for a few seconds. It felt good to laugh after the stress we had just gone through.

"Well, we can track water; that's easy," Michael continued, becoming serious once again. "Using imaging systems on the subjects, and recording the paths, we were able to finish the map. And not just lines on a piece of paper, but actual 3-D models of the bridges and pathways—an electrical diagram of the brain, if you will."

"That's pretty cool, but what does that have to do with Neola?" Dad asked.

"I'm getting to that," Michael said. "Just bear with me for a minute. As I was saying, we had the map. Our goal was to use that to help people with Amyotrophic lateral sclerosis or ALS, as well as Alzheimer's, dementia, and so on. However, we noticed something strange when we increased magnification on the bridges. Some areas of the brain had stubby arbors that branched off, disconnected and led to nothing. We found this to be the case in known healthy patients as well as diseased patients. We zoomed out our scan's magnification some and found those stubs had corresponding stubs directly across the vast space from each other. We concluded that the connection of those bridges existed at one point in time, but because of disease, lack of use, or even environmental exposure, the connections had died and broken. We found the same thing in our rodent test subjects. Once we connected the bridges, areas of the brain previously dark lit up in the MRI and became active. We knew from earlier studies by another division of EnGen, that those same areas that became active in our test mice were areas that were only active in human subjects having special abilities, such as clairvoyance, telepathy, and even psychokinesis.

"From there, the studies progressed. My partner, Dr. Julie Gibbs, reconnected each arbor in the 3-D model to create a completely connected map in the software. Then we began to re-create the brain in the lab using stem cells from mice that had all the bridges reconnected. We were successful, and more areas of that brain lit up than we had ever seen before," Michael said and sat there staring at the firelight for a minute before he finally looked up. "Neola is the first and only result of those tests on a human subject."

"So what are you saying?" I asked. "Connecting those pathways gave her the ability to talk to strange cats?"

"Yes," Michael answered. "But that's not all. We don't really know yet what all she can do. Let me explain it this way. Do you know the Bible stories we were told as children about Adam and Eve in the garden?" He looked up at Dad and me. We both nodded. "Well," he continued, "they were said to be perfect, newly created by God. If that were true and they were perfect, they would've had all these arbors, sorry, bridges, connected. Then the theory is that they had many abilities, to include being able to talk to each other in their minds, as well as to God.

When they started having children, and those children had children, they began to get farther and farther from perfect creation, and their bodies began to degrade, becoming not so perfect.

"Now here we are thousands of years later. The human body and brain has changed, or evolved due to exposure to such things as disease, environmental factors, pesticides and chemicals. Everything changed the body at the genetic level. We evolved negatively. I'm not talking about the levels of evolution, but a level of change within a shorter period of time. That we do know."

"I don't know if I've ever met a scientist who talked about the Bible in such a way as to make me think he believed the biblical account," Dad said.

"I don't know, maybe." Michael said. "Based upon what I have witnessed throughout this program, and what I have seen in Neola, there has to be a higher level of intelligence. How could the brain be so complicated and have the ability to do what it does, and what we think it can do, fully remapped? How could that be by chance, just happen by accident? However, my comparison wasn't because I believe or not, but just one example of how the brain could have undergone degradation over human existence."

"So you guys operated on Neola, reconnecting the bridges in her brain?" I asked. "How did you do that? It must've taken forever."

"No," Michael said, "she was genetically engineered."

"What does that mean?" I asked.

"You must've heard of stem cells, right?"

"Yes, I have."

"Well, that was just the beginning of it when it started back in the early part of the twenty-first century. It has progressed to now being able to grow any organ for transplant. As you know, there are banks that have stores of hearts, lungs, kidneys; you name it, for those who paid to have a backup grown for them. They just need tissue and the genetic code. Well, even the growth of a brain is possible, though it would be impossible to surgically replace one. Once we were able to completely map the brain, we then grew it fully mapped through genetic sequencing. Once we did that, we were able to put that genetic code into an embryo and grow it into a fully functioning person."

"Neola is from a test tube?" Dad asked.

"Not technically, we don't call it that anymore, but yes she was grown and raised in a lab," Michael responded.

"Does she know?" I asked.

"Yes, I told her everything when we ran away," Michael said. "It was the hardest thing I ever had to do. She took it well. She's very smart, and I think she knew deep down. Please don't hold that against her. She is as much a person as you and I."

"So what was it EnGen wanted from this experiment, with Neola?" Dad asked. "What was her future if you stayed there? In other words, why did you finally decide to kidnap her and leave?"

"She's exactly why we left," Michael responded. "The program started out as medical science in hopes of understanding and maybe curing some of the neurological disorders, but ended up turning into a military project.

They were pushing us to take it to the next level. They wanted us to figure out what she could do and train her how to control it. She would have been the first of many. Then, they were going to take her and train her to be a spy or assassin. Mr. Roberts, the head of the project, wants to build a small army of assassins like Neola. He feels they would be invaluable in stopping terrorism.

"You see, at the age of twelve he lost his parents in the attacks of September 11, 2001, back when this was the United States. They both were in the first tower when it came down. He grew up angry and vowed to be a part of the organization that rid the world of the group involved in the attacks, and anyone who supported them. With Neola's progress and her abilities growing stronger, he felt he finally had found something invaluable to help the fight. This is why he so wanted the project to succeed.

"I didn't want any of that for her, so I destroyed as many of the records I could of Neola and the program. Only a secure filing room that I didn't have access to contains the remaining lab notes, studies, and test papers. I wish I could have gotten to those. Dr. Gibbs had already destroyed all the electronic files, which is why they moved the paper documents and secured them."

"So, what all can she do?" I asked. "I mean, what abilities does she have?"

"We don't really know. I mean, we found she could read minds. She can also move small objects with her mind, even bend a spoon and those types of abilities. And we were just figuring out more when we left. We were testing her to see if she could control someone else's mind, but had not been successful, until this evening. We don't know what all she can do beyond that. We can only imagine. No one has gotten this far. She is only in the infancy of her training and abilities."

"Are you going to continue to train her?" Dad asked.

"I'm torn on that," Michael said. "If I don't train her, she may have a somewhat normal life. However, if the company finds her, she will be unable to defend herself. If I do train her, she will likely not have anything close to a normal life, but again, at least she will be able to defend herself and protect those she cares about."

"So what now?" I asked.

"We get as far away from the company and this 'sanctuary' as possible. Eventually, I want to go to another country. That's why we were in the transport hangar. Those airplanes were headed to Great Britain. We hoped to sneak out when the ship landed and disappear."

"And we messed up those plans, didn't we?" Dad said.

"Yes, but it wasn't your intention. Once the ship's crew knew people were in the hangar, they would have discovered us, even if your family escaped. They would have searched the hangar until they were sure no one else was there. We had to leave. You became our escape."

We talked for a little while longer, until we decided to go to sleep. The three of us let Mom, Neola, and my brothers sleep in the airplane, while we slept on the ground next to the fire. Knowing those cats were out there was a little unnerving. I didn't know what time I finally fell asleep. I was exhausted.

I awoke to the sound of birds chirping. The sun's light

rays made their way through the tree branches and shined directly on my face. I sat up. I noticed Michael and Neola over with one of the cats. It turned and walked away. As Michael and Neola came back to the almost—extinguished fire, Michael looked at my dad and me and said, "We sent them away instructing them not to bother us."

"That's good," I said. "They're scary looking. And I don't like knowing they're out there around the camp."

"They won't be any more," Neola said. "I told him to go to the other side of the sanctuary for the day."

"They did say there were some wild berries and fruit trees about a mile south of here," Michael said. "We should get moving. If we can make it there and get something to eat, the fence is a short distance beyond that. There's a section where the fence runs over some rocks, and we should be able to squeeze under without touching it."

"The cats told you that?" I asked.

"Yes, basically," Neola answered. "And there's an office building with vehicles we can borrow."

"Well, let's get the gear and head out," Dad said.

"Let's be on our toes though," Michael said. "We still don't know what else is out there."

# CHAPTER 16

**Looking at the wreckage again, it was a miracle** everyone survived.

"Let's head out," Dad said.

We gathered up everything we felt would come in handy and headed off into the forest. We walked single file, dodging limbs, pushing ferns aside, and stepping over rocks. No one talked. The woods were dark in areas from the thick, lush plants and trees. Our eyes struggled to focus. We made our way downhill, sometimes following trails left by animals. Dad led with Mom and my brothers behind him, followed by Michael, Neola, and me at the rear. With no water left, I was beginning to get thirsty. Already starved, I hoped we would find the fruit trees soon. I really just wanted to get out of this place.

Parker and Zach were arguing with each other about something. They were tired. I don't think anyone had gotten much sleep.

"It's mine. I saw it first," Zach said.

"No, it's mine," Parker said. "I found it."

"Gimme it!" Zach said, pulling something from Parker's hand.

"Mom!" Parker said.

"What are you two fighting about?" Mom asked. "Give me that, Zach."

"It's mine, though. I found it."

"Let me see it."

Zach reached out and handed it to Mom. As I stepped up, Mom was holding what looked to be a piece of the cat's armor. It was square and looked like a hard bone or something.

"It must have come loose when I stuck the cat with the spear," I said.

"Boys, I will hold onto this for now." Mom told them and put it in her pocket.

At last we came to a clearing. On the other side, we saw a couple of apple trees and some wild blackberry bushes. The cats were right.

Excited, we all seemed to race each other across the field, unintentionally at first. Each taking notice that the others were speeding up, we all began to run. My brothers were pretty quick. They had the most fun, it seemed, although Mom and Neola were laughing and trying to beat them. It was the first time I'd heard laughter from my family in quite a while.

We made it to the fruit and ate more than we probably should have; some of us might regret it later.

"This tastes so good," I said.

"I know," Mom said. "I'm so hungry."

"I don't think I've ever had blackberries before," Neola said. "They are my new favorite."

"I knoow! Soooo goood," Parker said with a full mouth barely comprehendible.

We laughed. Then we stuffed as many apples as we could into our bags and prepared for the last hike to the fence.

"Is everyone ready to move on?" Dad asked. Everyone said yes. "Well, let's go. Follow me." We started toward the fence.

"Look, Dad," Zach said, pointing toward the clearing. "Are those wolves?"

We all turned around and saw about five wolves at the far edge of the clearing just inside the tree line. They appeared to be preparing to cross the clearing after us, slightly hidden in the shadows, sniffing the ground.

"Everyone, back away slowly," Dad ordered. "Don't run or let them see you turn around. When we get down the hill and out of their sight, we will turn around and run," Dad finished his instructions as he pulled out his 9mm pistol. He released the clip. "Only three," he mouthed to Michael and me. Michael squinted at Dad, realizing he had lied last night about having a weapon.

We were far enough into the trees and out of the wolves' sight. "Now turn, run! Michael can you lead us toward that tall tree in the distance? Brad and I will follow in the rear," Dad said.

As we started to run, the wolves began to howl, but only for a few seconds before they went silent. "They're coming!" Dad said.

The clearing was probably a hundred yards across but wouldn't have taken the wolves too long to sprint it. We were rushing through the underbrush. As Neola made her way through, a branch sprung back and smacked me in the face. Forced to back off some, I held my arms up in front of my face to protect my eyes. As we ran, I just knew the wolves were on our heels. I continued to look back, worried about Dad but also checking to see if I could spot them. *Nothing yet!*

Then, out of nowhere, we heard barking or yelping not only behind us, but also beside us. They must've been talking to each other. We continued to run. The fence appeared in front of us, tall from our perspective down here on the ground. Flying over it, I had not realized its size.

"Almost there," I yelled. There was a small clearing between the forest and the fence, a safety zone of some sort. As we came out of the trees and started across the small clearing, I saw wolves exit the trees on both sides of us, as if boxing us in. I looked behind me, but Dad never came out.

"Dad!" I yelled. As a started back in, pulling my knife out of my pocket, there was a gunshot. "Dad!" I said again as I ran into the trees. Everything imaginable that could have happened was running around in my head.

About 20 yards in, there he was with a dead wolf lying on top of him. His pants were torn and his left leg was bleeding. I dragged the wolf off of him. I started to help him up when we heard a growl. To our left stood another wolf showing his teeth. Then I heard another one to our right. They were slowly approaching us.

"Dad, give me the gun!" I said as I reached for it. One wolf was closer than the other, so I pointed the gun at it. They crept forward, teeth gnashing. The one I chose to shoot was snapping its jaw as it growled. It seemed highly aggressive, and I was sure it wasn't going to back down. Holding Dad up, we slowly backed away. I gently squeezed the trigger, with the sights aimed directly between its eyes. Just as the gun went off, Dad lost his balance pulling me to the side.

I missed where I was aiming, but I must've still hit the wolf, because it yelped and took off running in the opposite direction. It continued to yelp as it moved farther into the woods. The gunshot and yelping must have frightened the other wolf, because it too turned and ran. Together Dad and I headed toward the fence.

"We can cross here," Michael said. He had found a good spot to go under the fence and had already made it to the other side. "But you must not contact the fence. It will zap you good."

The remaining two wolves were close to Mom and the others when we came out of the trees and started across the open space to the fence. The wolf that ran off scared didn't run far. It stood right behind us at the tree line. A little more skittish, it kept its distance. Slowly backing toward the fence, Dad and I faced the wolf. The other two wolves turned their focus on us. Dad was injured and would make easier prey.

"Joanne, get the boys under the fence," Dad said. "Now!"

Dad only uses Mom's name when he is serious. We were all scared, and dad was hurt and of little help right now. That must've made him more nervous.

Neola was already making her way under the fence.

"Can't you do something?" I asked her. "Order them to leave or something."

"I can't," she said.

"Why?" I asked.

"She can't because they're just dumb animals," Michael said. "The cats had human DNA in them. These don't appear to."

With Neola completely through the hole under the fence, my brothers started through one at a time. Mom helped them under, ensuring they didn't contact the fence, as Neola pulled from the other side. Dad and I still backed up, trying not to move too fast and encourage the wolves to attack. I held the pistol up, ready just in case, one bullet remaining.

With teeth showing, the growling wolves inched closer and closer. There we were, three wolves and only one bullet. I knew I had to wait until the moment was right. If I shot too early the other two may spook but come back before Dad and I made it under the fence.

Looking over my shoulder, my brothers were through and Mom was starting to shimmy under.

"Hurry!" I yelled. "They're getting too close."

"Michael, find a rock to roll in place once we make it through," Dad said. "We don't want these wolves following us under."

"I'm on it."

"Joanne," Dad continued. "You and Neola collect a handful of smaller rocks that you can throw at the wolves if they do start to get through the fence before Michael plugs the hole."

The wolf on my left started to move forward quicker than the other two. It was only 10 feet away.

"Get back!" I yelled, stomped, and swung my arms at the wolf. Letting go of Dad so abruptly caused him to stumble and almost fall. The wolf stopped and jumped back a few steps in fear, but only for a second before it continued toward us again. I caught Dad's arm in time to keep him on his feet. As we approached the fence, I let him go and he started under the fence.

The three wolves slowed their steps as if preparing to pounce. Mom helped Dad through the fence, to safety on the other side. Only I remained.

"Get ready," I said. "I'm going to shoot this one in front of me and hope the other two are scared enough to give me time to crawl under."

"Ready when you are son," dad answered.

Stopped, I was backed up to the fence. The wolves were within eight feet of me, also standing still. Teeth bared, all three of them were now snapping their jaws. They had a low hiss to their growl. Their eyes stared at me as they drooled with hunger. My heart pounded in fear. They were preparing to attack.

The two on either side of me were gray and not as big as the black one who was eyeing me straight on. I had to get under the fence but was scared to make my move. *What if the other two didn't scare when I shot the black one?* I thought. They would definitely attack and I wouldn't make it, certainly not without touching the electric fence. Aiming at the wolf, I held my breath and prepared to fire.

I really didn't want to shoot, but there was no other

way. Easing back on the trigger, the gun went off. I didn't know exactly where I hit the wolf, but it jumped back, yelped, and fell to the ground kicking and whining. I was saddened. I looked at the other two, which turned and ran only about 10 feet toward the trees before slowing down. I made my move, toward the opening, crawling as quickly as I could. The two wolves turned toward me. They charged the fence. They were coming fast. They were at the fence just as I pulled my feet under. I felt contact on my left shoe and jerked my foot away. I rolled onto my side and away from the hole.

"Now!" Dad yelled. Mom and Neola threw rocks into the gap under the fence as Michael released the large rock. It rolled toward the hole. One of the wolves' heads was halfway under the fence when the rock crashed into it. With a yelp, it jumped back as sparks flew from its contact with the fence. From the impact of the rock and the shock from the fence, it fell back dazed. Getting up, it stood next to the other one, growling at us as they eyed our every move. The safety of the fence separated us.

"Are you OK?" Mom asked me as she bent down to my side.

"I'm fine," I said to her. "Dad, how are you?" I asked him looking at his still-bleeding leg.

"I'll live. We should probably clean and dress this, though," he answered pointing to the gnarly gash in his leg.

"Let's get up over these rocks and away from the fence so the wolves will move on," Mom said. "They're creeping me out."

# CHAPTER 17

**We made our way out of sight** of the fence and prepared to take care of Dad's wound using the first-aid kit Neola grabbed from the airplane. A few minutes of rest benefited everyone.

"Mom, that was scary,' Parker said.

"Yeah, it was," Zach added.

"It's OK now," Mom said as she grabbed them, one in each arm and pulled them close to her.

"We're safe now," I said to them, ruffling their hair as I walked past to go sit by Neola.

Mom and Michael began to work on Dad's leg, cleaning and covering the wound. The bite was deep and looked as though the wolf's teeth had nicked dad's shinbone. *I sure hoped they could get it cleaned up so it didn't become infected.*

"You're going to want to get a tetanus shot and maybe even a rabies vaccine soon," Michael said to Dad as they wrapped his wound.

"I'll check, but I'm sure I'm up on all my shots since I have flown to different countries for the company. Thank you for helping with my leg, though," Dad said.

"How are you doing?" I asked Neola as I sat down

beside her.

"OK, I guess. I just wish this was all over and we could finally find somewhere safe.

"Yeah, me too. But from what it sounds like, Michael doesn't believe that will happen until someone destroys the lab notes, journals, and printed files."

"I don't know if that will be possible."

"Why?"

"Well, just being able to get in there past all the security, locate the files, and destroy them, it just seems impossible."

"With your abilities, we just might be able to figure out a way," I said trying to lift her spirits.

"We?" She asked.

"Sure, I want to help."

"Really?"

"Yes."

"But, I don't know how much help even I can be," she said.

"What else can you do besides convincing people and freakish cats to do what you want them to do?" I asked with a smile.

"Hand me that small rock there."

"This one here?" I asked picking up a rock about an inch in size.

"Yes, now hold it in your right hand, with your palm up and open."

I held up my hand and opened my fist, the rock exposed in the center of my palm. Without warning, it lifted off my hand and floated over into Neola's open hand a few feet away. I looked at her in amazement.

"That's so cool! How big of an object can you move?"

"Not much bigger than this. They said I should be able to move larger items if I really focused and believed. Michael said a person could move a mountain if they had enough faith in where their power comes from."

"I've heard that as well, but it seems hard to believe," I said. She made the rock float back to me. I grabbed it out of the air.

"Now, please open your hand again."

I did. The rock shot out of my hand so fast it somewhat burnt my skin as it slid across it. It flew with great speed through the open space until it hit a tree 20 yards away.

"That was awesome!" I said. "What else can you do? This is cool!"

"That's it really," she replied and looked down. "I feel like a failure. I keep trying, but it is so hard."

"We'll figure it out and will use it to destroy the lab notes." I said. "You're not a failure, far from it."

Neola smiled as I looked into her eyes for a brief moment before she bashfully looked away.

"So," I continued, "where do you live when you're at the lab?"

"Actually, I lived in a glass room built in the corner of the lab. There were cameras everywhere."

"Everywhere?" I asked.

Knowing what I was meaning, she said, "I had a curtain in the bathroom to hide me, as well as one in the bedroom to change behind."

"That still would've sucked knowing someone was watching you all the time."

"Not really, I grew up with it and that was all I knew."

"What did they do to you there, if you don't mind me asking?"

"I remember when I was younger, they used to test me with games and toys," she started. "For example, they had these flashcards with pictures on them. They would pull one out and asked me what the picture was on it, but not show me. At first, I would be close, but later I would start getting it right. At age six, I never missed another card."

"Clairvoyance?" I asked.

"They thought that, and at first maybe so. By the time I was eight, I think I saw the card because they saw the card."

"You were reading their mind."

"Yes, but back when I was eight, I wasn't sure that's what I was doing. I think it wasn't until I was around eleven when I realized I was reading their minds. It was nice to know what they were thinking. I learned quickly who cared for me and who didn't. But I didn't tell them for a while, worried about how they would take it when they learned I could read their thoughts, afraid they might hurt me."

"Yeah, I can see that. They couldn't keep a secret from you any longer and would no longer have the upper hand."

"They found out in the end, just before we left. That's one of the reasons we did leave."

"Sorry, this whole thing just isn't right," I said putting my hand on her hand feeling sad for her life. She looked up when I did. We sat there eye to eye, for what seemed like forever. I became lost in her beautiful eyes again. Finally knowing I should look away, I broke the silence and asked, "Do you read people's minds often?"

"Are you asking me if I have read your mind or if I'm reading your mind right now?" she asked, grinning a little.

"No, not really." I responded feeling my face flush some. I didn't want her knowing I was thinking about her, what I thought of her.

"Not very often," she answered. "And no, I'm not reading your mind. I did once, but that was back in the hangar. I looked into you and your Dad before Michael approached you to be sure you were safe."

"What did you see in me?"

"That you were kind. You seem like a good person," she said bashfully. "You were scared, worried about your family. You seemed safe."

"That was the only time you did that?"

"Yep. As far as I know anyway. Michael thinks sometimes I may do it out of self-defense, not even knowing it."

"I think that's true because back when we were fighting the cats, I heard a voice in my head that told me about the vulnerable spot on the cat's belly. I think that was you reading their thoughts, knowing their vulnerability, and passing it along to me. Do you remember that? Or is that something you may have been doing without realizing it?"

"I don't remember doing it," she said.

"Well, how do you not do it?" I asked. "I mean, how hard is it to control—to turn on and off?"

"It's pretty easy now. Before, I just heard all these voices in my head. I thought I was going crazy. Once I figured out what they were, I had to focus hard on each voice to shut them off. Once I learned how to do it, then I had to focus to turn them back on. I can do it easy now, but I have to consciously want to. I have to think about it. People I know and trust, well I just don't turn it on anymore. The people I don't know, or don't trust, I don't feel guilty about it. If I need information, I will read their minds to get it. But again, only to protect either someone I care about or myself. That's how we found out where the lab notes and the other papers were."

"That's pretty cool," I said. "You also said there were games they tested on you?"

"Yes, different types of engineered puzzles and games to test my IQ and my analytical abilities. I guess to see if I could solve them and if so, how fast."

"How did you do?"

"Let's just say that by the time I was ten, there wasn't a puzzle or a test I couldn't figure out."

"Kids, we should probably get going," Dad said as he came up behind Neola and put a hand on each of our shoulders.

"OK, Dad," I said, looking at him. I looked back at Neola and said, "We will get to those notes and destroy them, I promise." I tried to sound confident, yet I wasn't truly sure how we would do it.

Neola stood there looking at my dad as he limped off favoring his wounded leg. I wondered what she was thinking but didn't say anything. She stood there for quite a while.

"Your dad overheard something when he worked at

EnGen, didn't he?" she asked.

"Yes, how do you know that?" I asked but realized I already knew the answer.

"No, I didn't read his mind. When he touched me, I saw it. Sometimes that happens."

"Well, he didn't tell us what he heard, trying to protect us, but he did say they would likely want to kill him for hearing it, tying up loose ends or something like that. Dad thinks they already killed his copilot and friend."

"Sorry," she said.

We collected our things and headed east, through the woods in the direction of the town we saw before we crashed the airplane. The sun was straight above us. My brothers were a little scared entering the woods again, after the wolves. We did our best to reassure them as we moved on. We had walked for about 30 minutes when Michael spotted what appeared to be a dirt road off in the distance. Hoping it would lead us to the highway and back to town, we headed toward it. We all felt a little relieved. Walking through the woods, not knowing where we were or if we would find a way out is not a good feeling.

Dad seemed to be walking better. His leg must not hurt as bad because he was keeping up with Michael's pace. We approached the dirt road and looked both directions before we walked out onto it. It extended in both directions until it faded into a corner each way and we could see no farther.

"Which way?" Michael asked.

"Not sure," Dad answered. "No telling where each direction leads. We were flying east toward town before we ran out of gas. It appeared the sanctuary was mostly to our north, so if we head north, it may lead us to the main EnGen building. From there, we could likely find the highway.

"But I want to stay as far away from them as possible," Michael said.

"I understand. We can follow the road, but from the cover of the woods," Dad suggested. "We would be out of sight. If we can find the highway and head back toward town, we could find shelter and maybe even a vehicle."

"OK," Michael relented. "But we stay in the woods and if we see something that may put Neola or any of us in danger, we head deeper into the woods."

"Agreed," Dad said. "You ready, honey?" he said to Mom, who had the boys beside her.

"How is your leg? Do you need to rest?" she asked.

"I'm fine. It feels much better," he answered. "We should keep moving."

"I am, too. I don't want to go toward them," Mom added. "I just don't trust that company after some of the stories you've told me. Do you really feel that's the only way for us to make it back to town?" she asked, holding onto my brothers, rubbing their shoulders. We could see her worry.

"I do. Any sign of trouble, or if there are too many people around for us to safely make it past the facility, we will turn back and go way around," Dad promised her.

"I trust you. Let's go, boys," she said as she squeezed the twins while looking at me with her "I love you" smile, something only Mom can do.

We started to step off the road, but Michael paused as he turned to Neola. He looked at her, concerned for her safety, from being that close to the very people they were running from. She stood there with him. He smiled and said, "It will be OK." She smiled back. Then, instantly her smile faded.

"Look out!" she screamed sensing something coming in fast just as it struck Michael in the chest. As he buckled over, the sound of a gunshot followed. We looked down the road to where the sound came from. Hundreds of yards down the road, a man was standing beside a Hummer with a rifle. He was loading another round.

Neola and I helped Michael off the road and into the cover of the trees. We laid him down. I held my hand on the wound, applying pressure, which seemed to be wasted effort. He laid there struggling to breathe. Knowing he only had minutes, he tried to speak to Neola, who was sobbing at his side.

"Neola, hu-honey," he stuttered with pain. "Focus on ya-your powers, la-learning what you can do. Eh-imagine in your mind doing it, li-like I taught you. If y-you have the ability, you'll do it. Then go de-destroy the records of your existence. I-it is the only way you'll be fa-free."

"I will," Neola sobbed.

"Na-now you must go, leave me! They're coming and wa-wa-we're trespassing. Sa-sorry I cannot help you any longer."

"Don't talk like that, I can heal you," she said as she moved my hand and placed hers over the wound. She closed her eyes and concentrated. By this time, the internal bleeding was filling his damaged lungs and making its way into his mouth. He was coughing and spitting blood. He was going fast.

I could hear the Hummer heading our way, getting closer every second. Neola was still concentrating hard, starting to make the bullet exit. Michael winced in pain so she stopped.

"I-I love you," Michael said as he took his last breath.

Neola screamed. The Hummer approached. She caught sight of it. Without warning, the Hummer exploded, erupting in fire and debris. It startled us. We stumbled back from the force.

Neola looked down at Michael once again, streams of tears rolling down her cheeks.

"Honey, we must go," Dad said to her gently. "Brad, see if there are any survivors in the truck," he said to me as he helped Neola up. "Honey, take her," he said leading her into Mom's arms.

I ran over to the road. The Hummer was in pieces. There wasn't much left that would identify it as a Hummer. "Well, there aren't any survivors. I wonder if they had a bomb that went off."

"Not sure," Dad answered as he went through Michael's pockets.

"What are you doing?" I asked.

"If they figure out who he is, they will know Neola is near."

Just then, I heard another truck coming down the gravel road.

"Dad, another rig! Do you think they blew up the

Hummer?"

"I don't know, son, but let's go, now!" Dad ordered a bit too late. The vehicle was there and slid to a stop.

"Hold it right there!" The guard from the back seat said, pointing his rifle at us as he jumped out. "Drop your weapons!"

"We have no weapons." Dad said with his hands in the air.

"Don't lie to me!" he yelled. The driver and another man approached and stood beside the first, all pointing their assault rifles at us. "What happened to the Hummer? Now talk!"

"No, you stop talking!" Neola said as she stepped forward. "Put your guns down!" The men looked at each other. "Now!" she ordered, still crying. Without further hesitation, the men laid their guns on the ground.

"We're going to take your vehicle," Neola continued. "You men will dig a hole in the woods, with your bare hands, and bury my friend. You will not tell anyone where he is, or that anyone else was here. Then you'll come back here and clean up this mess. Pile every piece of metal from this destroyed vehicle next to the road, do you understand?"

"Yes, ma'am," they said in unison.

"We're leaving," she continued. "Now get to work!"

The men went over to Michael, picked him up and carried him off into the woods. Neola lost it again, and began to cry harder. Dad and I grabbed their rifles and helped everyone into the Hummer. We drove off. Dad drove as I attempted to figure out the GPS in the dash. No one spoke as we drove down the dirt road. Neola continued to cry.

# CHAPTER 18

**I was sitting in the passenger's seat, up front with Dad.**
Behind Dad sat Neola, with Mom and the boys beside her.
I would look back at Neola every so often to see how she
was holding up. She was distraught. Usually she was
looking down at the floorboard of the truck or out the
window. I felt so bad for her. Here was this girl who had
just found out she was not normal, had no family of her
own. Swept away from all she had known and told it was
for her own safety. Now to have lost the one person she
had any connection with.

Having her with us did add to the danger my family was
already in. But I didn't care. Something about her drew me
in. Not just her beauty, but something else. Her situation
maybe, where she came from, I'm sure. Between curiosity
and pity, I felt I must know more about her. I must help
her.

I must have been unintentionally staring at her while I
was in thought because she looked up at me. Her eyes were
red from crying. Realizing she saw me staring, I cracked a
small "pity" smile at her and then asked, "Are you OK?"
She just shook her head yes and looked back out the
window. She needed more time.

I finally figured out the GPS and found a way through the maze of gravel roads back to the highway. We turned and headed toward Portland. We were all getting hungry. Mom had Parker look under the seat to see what he could find. There was a flashlight, some flares, some miscellaneous tools, and a flat plastic tote. He dragged the tote out, working it between his feet and up onto their laps. He opened it and to our great relief, food!

"Wow!" Zach said. "Look at all the goodies."

It appeared to have been the men's lunch, snack, or even emergency stock. It might even have been their dinner. There were only three men in the vehicle, but there was enough food for twice that, and plenty for all of us. Most of the food was in sealed pouches, sort of a military pack. The packages had sandwiches like peanut butter and jelly, dehydrated meats, dried fruits and veggies, cookies, and even some desserts like apple pie. There were protein bars, eight small bottles of water, more food than we had seen in days. Even the sight of the food in the bin seemed to pick Neola up, lifting her spirits. She reached over and put her hand on a protein bar, looked up at mom and asked, "You mind if I have one of these?"

"No, honey, this is yours too, help yourself," she said with a smile. "What else would you like?"

"Just this for now, thanks."

Mom picked up a water bottle and handed it to her, knowing she needed, it too. "Here, boys," she said as she began to hand out the food to the rest of us. The excitement on my brothers' faces as they tore into the packages, like Christmas morning. We enjoyed the meal as if we were eating at a restaurant. The food lifted everyone's spirits. Since yesterday, we had not been sure when we were going to see food again. Even though we didn't know when the next time would be, we didn't care. We ate until our hearts, and stomachs, were content.

We drove for about an hour, making our way closer to the city. The vehicle's electric power was still going strong. The computer said the system had eight more hours of battery reserve before it would require a charge. Dad said the electric vehicles go much farther than they used to when they were first designed. "You know, son," Dad continued, "for a vehicle this large and heavy, it is impressive how fast and long this thing will go on batteries and an electric motor."

I just smiled at him. It didn't mean that much to me, but his nerdy side shone through sometimes. This was one of those times. You see, my dad used to be an engineer for a large aviation company. He got his pilot's license while working there and logged many hours test flying the airplanes off the production line. He eventually quit and took the job at EnGen as a lead pilot.

The city was drawing near. The quality and size of the road increased, as did the number of vehicles. Dad was still in manual driver's mode. He was old-fashioned and loved to drive. Most people just let the car drive itself on the roads, so much safer. In fact, there'd been a big push to make it illegal to drive manually within the city limits, not allowing the vehicles to come out of auto-drive mode.

As we approached the city, tall, odd-shaped buildings riddled the skyline. The greater the population the higher up the buildings had to go. To slow the population's growth, the government had started to regulate the number of children a couple could have. I'm just glad they hadn't started that until after Zach and Parker were born or we wouldn't have them with us. Two years after my brothers were born, the government limited the number of children to only two per couple. If twins were in the family tree within two generations on either side, couples could only have one child, if the first attempt was not twins. Since Mom's father was a twin, my parents would've had to stop with me, because if the second attempt at a child ended up being twins, it would put the total at three. The government requires a small microchip be embedded in the woman to prevent her from becoming pregnant after the second. If something happened to one of the first two children before their 18 birthday, the couple could choose to have the chip removed and conceive another child.

The traffic picked up. All kinds of sleek, full-window cars zipped past us with a hum. The styling of the cars made them appear to hover along the highway. They would switch lanes as they were going around us and speed by. Dad had to drive slower because of being in manual mode. The speed limit on the roads only pertained to those who chose to do their own driving. Auto-drive vehicles could go as fast as the occupants chose.

This Hummer was still a fun ride. With the selection of city mode on the computer, this thing's ride became so comfortable. It even put mom and my brothers to sleep.

Looking out the window and seeing people in their vehicles on the way into the city, I realized the cars today were so safe. People could even sleep while the car drove to their destination, a good way to pass the time during the commute, I guess. With most all cars in auto-drive, there just weren't the slowdowns and traffic jams there used to be. Dad said this generation doesn't know how nice they have it. I just have to chuckle at him when he says things like that. Parents always say they had it harder than their kids. Grandpa used to say he had to walk to school uphill both ways. I don't think anyone would be able to use that line again.

Lost in my thought, I wasn't really paying too much attention at first, but then noticed Dad looking a little nervous and watching the rearview mirror.

"What is it?" I asked him.

"It is probably nothing, but there seems to be a couple of suspicious vehicles behind us. They may be following us."

I looked back in the side mirror and saw two dark cars single file, staying behind us but in a different lane. If the cars were in auto drive, they would likely have passed us by now. In manual-drive mode, it is difficult to maintain the same speed. That meant they too were in manual mode, going the same speed as us, on purpose.

Dad sped up to see if he could pull away from them or if they also would speed up. We started to build a distance from them, but after a few moments the two cars seemed to catch up. They were following us.

We had no idea where we were going, but we didn't like them following. It meant we were in danger once again. Looking back at Neola, I saw that she laid her seat back and was sleeping. We didn't want to wake her or the twins, but Dad felt he needed to try to lose the two cars, especially if they were the same people who shot Michael. Our only hope was to get off the highway and lose them in the city. We were within the city limits, with buildings on either side of us. Off ramps directed traffic to various city streets.

Dad took the next exit, and we both looked back in the mirrors with anticipation.

"Don't get off. Don't get off," I said aloud. Sure enough, they did. They were following us. A couple of cars separated them and us, and Dad took that as an opportunity to try to lose them.

"How did they find us," I asked.

"They likely tracked us using the computer in this vehicle," he answered. "They own the vehicle and know the system's signature. Check the GPS computer and see if you can find the option to turn the tracking feature off. It might be a little late, but if we can lose them maybe we can stay lost."

We raced around corners, zipping past cars in auto drive. The Hummer's auto drive safety feature has to report to any other vehicle in the area that it's in manual-drive mode. Obvious as the other cars were getting out of our way, opening up the lane ahead of us. This made it harder to lose the two cars behind us.

While Dad did his best on the crowded street, I thumbed through the settings of the computer. After a minute or so, I finally found it: Allow Tracking. A checkmark in the box. I touched the box to remove the checkmark and hit save.

"There, got it," I said.

"Now, as long as they don't have access to turn it back on, if we lose them, we should be able to disappear," Dad said. "But we will need to get out and as far away from this vehicle as we can to be sure."

Our large vehicle wasn't the best for aggressive city driving. Because we had to slow down so much for the corners, the two cars chasing us caught up easily. We came to an intersection. Dad made an immediate left turn. Looking over at the passing office buildings, I saw the Hummer's reflection jumping from window to window.

Neola and Mom seemed to wake at the same time because Dad took the last corner faster than he had been now that the two cars were right behind us.

"What's the rush?" Mom asked, rubbing her eyes.

"We have a couple of cars following us," Dad answered.

"What do you mean?" she asked.

"Just before we entered the city, I spotted two suspicious cars keeping pace with us in manual drive," he said. "I became aware of them when they didn't pass, they hung back there."

"We think they were tracking the GPS," I added." We turned it off, so hopefully if we lose them, they won't find us again."

"Are they from EnGen?" Neola asked.

"I think so," Dad said. "And I think they know you're in here. They may have figured out it was Michael they killed. I don't think they know I'm in here. Won't that be a shocker?"

Neola turned around and looked at the cars behind us. She continued to stare back, sliding back and forth in her seat as Dad dodged slow-moving cars and around corners. She was focusing hard. After a few moments, she turned back around somewhat pouting. She seemed disappointed and confused.

"What's wrong?" I asked.

"I don't know why, but for some reason I can't reach them."

"What do you mean?" Mom asked.

"I tried to control them, to tell them to stop chasing us, but I can't find their thoughts. It is as if they're blocking me."

"They may have something that jams or interferes with your thoughts or ability to control them," Dad said. "Something their car is transmitting maybe. That proves they know you're here."

"Well, we'll just have to do it the old-fashioned way!" Dad added as he took a left turn without warning us, shooting between traffic. The two cars behind us had to pause until their path cleared, but it didn't create enough space between them and us. Dad was taking as many turns as he could in hopes of adding a few seconds' lead, throwing us back and forth in our seats.

Turning right on the next street, we saw traffic stopped ahead for a red light so pedestrians could cross the road.

"Now what?" I asked.

"Let's park," Dad said sarcastically as he jolted across traffic, taking a small gap between two vehicles and entering a parking garage.

The car behind us tried to make the same gap in traffic that we had, but didn't quite do it. Another car tried to stop but hit the back end of our pursuing vehicle, spinning it out of control. Still having forward momentum, it slid into the side of the parking structure. Dust and debris from the wall flew into the air and the car came to rest on the sidewalk. A miracle no one was hurt.

The second pursuing car slowed and made it past the traffic and into the garage behind us. Dad raced around the tight quarters as fast as possible. The tires squealed loudly on the smooth pavement at every turn. I worried he would hit the ceiling with the roof of our Hummer.

I was starting to get a little worried. *How were we going to lose them? If we wrecked, what would they do to Neola? What would they do to us?* I hoped we didn't have to find out.

The pursuing car was right behind us, better capable in these tight quarters than ours was. Dad continued up to the third level before he decided to take the down ramp in hopes of making it out the exit before the men from the first car could block it, if they were even OK.

Down we went, dodging cars on their way up.

"Look out!" I yelled. Rounding the corner, a car was backing out of a parking spot. The car wasn't out very far when we reached it. Dad cranked the wheel to the left in an attempt to go around it, but our front bumper clipped its back corner. The impact drove it back into its parking spot as it slammed against the wall. The Hummer jolted but handled the hit well, as if only scraping sagebrush on a desert run. We bounced some, but Dad regained control and continued toward the exit. The tires squealed as we hit the final down ramp toward the first level.

The car was right behind us. Effortlessly keeping up. The new Audi sportscar was made specifically for racing and high-performance driving. Our only chance was to cause this one to wreck as well.

Without any warning, a gunshot rang out. The bullet hit our front fender, ricocheting off the durable metal. The Hummer, designed to handle this type of abuse, wasn't fazed. Another shot rang out.

Dad locked his brakes. The Audi did the same but didn't hit us as Dad had hoped. Even though it was close to us, its stopping power was much greater than our heavy rig's. Gunning it, Dad squealed around the last corner before the exit came into sight.

We hit the exit ramp with such force that it sent us bouncing out onto the street; traffic split, swerving away from us as the cars in auto mode predicted our every move. The Audi came out right behind us. Unfortunately, we were on the wrong side of the road. Dad headed straight toward the oncoming cars. They swerved around us, likely the auto drive's anti-collision mode. Dad changed position between the two lanes, still heading in the wrong direction, in an effort to cause the cars to swerve into the pursuing Audi. It was unsuccessful.

Zach and Parker seemed to be enjoying the ride. They were smiling and giggling at each other as they bounced around. At least they didn't have any idea of the danger we were in. Mom, on the other hand, was scared. With each forceful turn, she would scream or make some kind of noise. She thought Dad drove too fast normally, always asking him to drive in auto mode. I could only imagine how she might have felt now.

Neola on the other hand, didn't seem too fazed by our speed and the sliding around. She just stared forward, holding onto the handle above her window keeping her in place. I wondered what she was thinking. Was she still upset by Michael's death and just didn't care about anything else right now, or was she scared by the driving and just didn't show it?

Dad swerved back to the other side of the road, realizing the cars in auto drive were avoiding the car chasing us and that he was causing unnecessary danger to us by heading into traffic. He took the most direct route, over the medium. The Hummer seemed to leave the road as we launched over the concrete medium. The low sportscar was unable to follow. We raced side-by-side, the sleek vehicle easily keeping pace.

The driver chasing us must have anticipated our move, taking the next available opening to cross the medium to our side of the road just as Dad tried to make a right turn. He was there with us, jolting across traffic.

The buildings flew by as we traveled speeds reserved for the highways. We knew it was only a matter of time before we attracted the attention of the authorities and, as expected, sirens erupted as a patrol car pulled in behind the Audi. It neither stopped us from fleeing, nor the Audi from chasing. We hoped it would discourage our pursuants and allow us to escape.

So there we were, the three of us, one after the other,

flying down the street avoiding cars and pedestrians. Right turn, left turn, oh crap, stoplight! Traffic stopped ahead of us. Dad took to the sidewalk, honking his horn as a couple dove out of the way. The Audi and the patrol car slowed to hop the curb the Hummer had taken easily.

Leaving the sidewalk, the Audi chased us while the patrol car chased it, none of us willing to stop. It was only a matter of time before more patrol cars joined in. Dad made turn after turn in order to make it harder for the other patrol cars to pinpoint us.

Up ahead, a city bus crawled in the right lane. We were in the left lane fast approaching.

"Hold on!" Dad said to everyone as he sped up.

Just passing the bus, he changed lanes when we were ahead of it. The Audi and the patrol car were still beside the bus. Dad took the next right. His hope was to use the bus to block the Audi's turn. It nearly worked, too, but the Audi floored it and cut off the bus, just making the turn, or so it appeared. At the last second, the Audi spun out, sliding into the rear end of a parked car. Its back right corner slightly bumped the bus, sending it into a slide. With the force started as it began to make the turn, contact with the bus sent it spinning.

Swerving left to miss the Audi, yet unsuccessful, the bus came to a stop pinning it in place against the curb. The Audi's driver hit his steering wheel with both hands in anger. His car was not going anywhere. The wheels against the curb looked bent by the weight and force of the bus pushing against it. The bumper of the bus smashed the driver's side door in, leaving the Audi driver trapped in his car because the passenger's side door was against a sign pole. I had to chuckle as I read the sign hanging on the pole just above the Audi: Safely Arrive in Auto Drive.

The bus blocked the road from everyone behind it, even the cop, allowing us to escape. Forced to stay there because of the wreck, the patrol car didn't follow us. Finally, the chase was over.

"Is everyone OK?" Dad asked as he slowed.

"Yes," we all answered

"Now that the police are involved," Dad said, "we need to get out of this Hummer,"

Turning a few more times to change directions, getting us farther out of the area of the wreck, Dad slowed and pulled over. He shut off the engine and popped the hood.

"Let's go," Dad ordered. "Grab as much stuff as you can. Honey, would you collect all we have left of the food," he said to Mom.

We emptied out the Hummer, leaving only the guns, pushing them under seats and out of sight. Dad was under the hood when we finished collecting everything.

"What are you doing?" I asked.

"Pulling the fuses so they can't track the vehicle's location," Dad said as he closed the hood and locked the doors. He dropped the keys into the nearest trash can. We headed down the sidewalk, blending into the crowd. We were safe, or at least for now... *But, where would we go?*

# CHAPTER 19

**We headed out of the center of town, walking on busy** sidewalks. We passed all types of people in all types of clothes, each accepted for exactly who they wanted to be and how they wanted to look. Face painting was the fad. Around their eyes and sometimes down their cheeks, people would paint their emotions.

A tall man in his mid-20s walked by with white painted around his eyes, in a circle. Below each eye were a nose and a smiling mouth painted in full color, a permanent smile. A woman about the same age walked just behind him with a triangle painted around her right eye in purple-and-white polka dots. The dots extended from around her eye, down to her jaw just in front of her ear, and forward to the center of her chin, forming a half moon to her mouth. The dots turned from a round shape to teardrops. She looked sad.

A group of teen girls about my age walked past with all sorts of painted patterns. They all looked at me and giggled as they discussed something among themselves.

"Have you seen all this before?" I asked Neola.

"No, I haven't," she replied. "Why do they paint their faces like that?" she said, wrinkling her nose.

"To be different I guess; to stand out. It is sort of like picking out clothes. We pick out and buy clothes we like, that fits our style and personality. I guess the idea is the same.

"Oh, I don't think I would do it."

"Me neither."

A woman was walking toward us, probably in her late 30s, and was looking straight ahead minding her own business. The next thing I knew, Neola had stepped in front of her. The woman stopped and then stepped to the side to try to get around her. Neola stepped with her and cut her off.

"Is there a problem?" the woman asked Neola, sounding a little angry.

"I'm sorry about your husband," Neola said.

"Excuse me?" The woman asked.

"Your husband Jack, leaving you."

"How do you know that? Who are you?"

"You think he left you for another woman, ran off, but he didn't. He needs you. You have to find him and help," Neola continued without answering her questions.

"What are you talking about?"

"There was an accident. On his lunch break, he went out to buy your anniversary present. Somebody mugged him while he was on his way back to his office. Stolen were his wallet, and the earrings he bought you. He let the robber take everything, up until the point when the man tried to take the earrings. He fought back. There was a scuffle and the robber knocked him down. He hit his head on the brick wall, hard. Somebody discovered him and called the ambulance. He was taken to General Memorial Hospital, where he is right now."

"Oh my gosh," the woman said, crying. "How do you..., nevermind. I've got to get to him!"

"One more thing before you go. He has amnesia. He doesn't remember who he is and he does not remember you. He needs you to help him remember. I want you to know he will remember you. It will take some time, but he will. He does love you."

"Thank you. Thank you so much, whoever you are," the woman said, bewildered, and took Neola by the hand. Letting go, she took off in a hurry, running toward the hospital. After about five steps, she stopped and turned around. "What is your name? I want to know your name."

"Neola," she yelled. "My name is Neola."

The woman stared at her for a moment before she smiled, turned and disappeared into the crowd. We all just stood and watched her disappear, amazed at what had taken place. Neola turned around and saw we were all staring at her.

"What?" Neola said smiling. "She was sad. She needed my help."

"No way! That was awesome!" I said. "Seriously amazing! How did you do that?"

"I don't know. Sometimes I just see things."

"Hey, let's stop here for a moment. I need to check our credits," Dad said as Neola and I talked about what had just happened.

We were at a bank. The information screen was set up to tell a person how many credits they had. No more withdrawing money these days because printed money no longer existed. Credits was the new term for money. With the joining of some nations together as one, the dollar, the pound and a few other accepted currencies combined into credits. A person earned credits working and then used them to buy things. We were low on credits since Dad had not been working these past few months. He wanted to see what we had left, for food and a place to stay. Before the whole trapped-in-the-hangar issue, we were staying at the abandoned airport out of town because we didn't have many credits left and we still couldn't go home. Dad placed his thumb on the glowing pad. The display read, "John Walker – credits = 514".

"Well, that's not enough to really do anything," Dad said. "Maybe a motel for the night and a little bit of food, but that's it."

"Can I check mine?" Neola asked. "Michael said he transferred some credits to me and told me to use them if we ever got separated, but I don't know how many."

"Sure, honey," Dad answered. "Come on up."

Dad stepped back to give her some privacy as she approached the machine. "Here?" she asked, pointing to the glowing thumb pad.

"Yes," I said and stepped up to help if she needed it. As I approached, she placed her thumb onto the pad. The display flickered and then displayed her information.

"What does this mean?" she asked. "Does that number mean the amount of credits I have in my name?"

"Yes," I said standing there in shock.

"Michael said he and Dr. Gibbs transferred credits to

me in hopes of it one day helping me to be free, but I didn't think it was that much." I looked back at Dad, who stepped up to the screen. It read "Neola Brandt - credits = 6,100,399.28". "They must've transferred their life savings to me. Why?" she said as her voice cracked. "And he gave me his last name. I didn't know that," she added. A tear slid down her face.

"It seems they did truly want you to have a normal life," Dad said, placing his hand on her shoulder.

We stood there for a few moments giving Neola a chance to absorb all of it. I wondered what she was thinking.

"Let's go sweetie," Dad said as he led Neola down the steps and into mom's arms.

"There, there," mom said as she embraced Neola, who was now bawling.

I felt so bad for her. To find out they had done something like this for her and she wasn't able to thank them for it would make it even harder to deal with.

"Let's get you out of here and find a quiet place to stay for the night," Dad said to her. "I want to get out of the city's center."

We left the bank and headed down the sidewalk. Neola, still emotional, walked silently, but looked around in apparent amazement, checking out the city. I was sure it was a completely new experience for her. It must have been overwhelming. All the people, each different in their own way, all the buildings, various shapes and sizes, the cars buzzing by, even the environment and not being in her small glass room she'd told me about. Everything must look so big and wonderful to her.

As people walked by, she really seemed to study them, even turning around to watch them walk past. Everyone so different, and so free; it must have been so strange to her.

We walked for what seemed like miles, down busy streets and through city parks, unsure of our destination.

"Mom, I'm tired," Zach said. "Can we rest?"

"Yeah, me too," Parker added. "How much farther?"

"Not much," she answered, looking over at Dad. "Right, honey?"

"No, just a few more blocks," Dad answered. "I have a place in mind."

We finally reached the motel Dad was taking us to. It was older, but newly remodeled. The front of the building only displayed windows with a main entrance in the middle identified by a sign. The vacancy light on the neon sign high above the building was lit up.

"You know about this place?" Mom asked him. "It's kind of out of the way."

"I stayed here years ago. I had a business meeting around the corner. It was a nice little place then, and I figured it would be a good place for us to lay low for the evening. Let's go check in. Then I can go find something for us to eat."

"Should we hide until you get the room?" Mom asked. "I'm only asking because of the car chase and the police."

"No honey, I don't think that will be necessary." Dad answered. "The police wouldn't know who was in the Hummer. The men chasing us wouldn't tell them because they want to find us themselves. We should be OK."

We all walked into the lobby and across the foyer to the front desk. It was clean and tidy; it appeared the owners took pride in their place. A tall skinny man in his mid-30s stood behind the counter. He was wearing a white button-up shirt with the motel's name embroidered on it. He had neatly combed hair. He smiled as we approached the counter. "Hello, how may I help you this evening?"

"How much for two rooms for the night?" Dad asked.

"That would be 500 credits," he answered.

"500, really? Prices sure have gone up. We'll take just one room then," Dad said.

"Oh, I'm sorry, we only allow five people per room. Insurance will not allow us to put six in one room."

"What?" Dad said.

"Sorry," the man said.

Dad looked back at Mom, who shrugged.

"I'll get it," Neola said as she stepped up to the counter. "It's the least I can do."

"Thumb here," the man said pointing to the red glowing light on the counter. It had a plastic housing in the shape of the thumb. Neola started to reach her thumb to the sensor when Dad called out, "Stop!" Neola jumped and everybody turned to look at him.

"Sorry to startle you, Neola," Dad said to her. "When do you charge the account?" Dad asked, looking at the man behind the counter.

"Not until checkout," he answered. "We just verify funds now. If there are sufficient funds, it will not charge until checkout, just in case you purchase movies, Internet, or that sort of thing. That way, we only bill you one time."

"Well, there should be no problems with funds," Dad said chuckling. "Go ahead, it's OK." Neola placed her thumb onto the sensor.

"OK, you're all set," the man said looking up at Neola as the sensor beeped in acceptance. "Your rooms are 115 and 116. I gave you adjoining rooms with a lockable inside door between the two if you want to easily move between them," he added as he handed the keys to Neola.

"Thank you," she said. "You should visit your mom. She misses you," she added, then turned to leave the lobby.

The man stood dumbfounded.

We found our rooms and settled in with Mom, Neola and my brothers in one, and Dad and me in the other. Mom thought it was best if Neola stayed with her and me with Dad. She thought it wouldn't be appropriate for the two of us to be in the same room. Like we would do anything, I had said to her. We opened the adjoining door. I think it was to help Dad feel more comfortable about our separation from them, even if only by a few feet.

The rooms had queen-size beds and a hide-a-bed, that with a flip of a switch, would automatically extend out of the wall. My brothers loved playing with it until Mom put a stop to it. There was a touch screen on the wall for Internet and movies, as well as local programming. The very end of the room had a sliding glass door that lead to the patio area containing a small table and two chairs each. The patios overlooked a large grassy park. Picnic tables and freestanding barbecues were ready for use, protected from the sun under the outstretched branches of a large oak tree.

I unlocked the sliding glass door, stepped out onto the patio, and sat down. I stared off into the grassy landscape thinking about the day. What a rush! First, the airport, then the flying suit, and then the plane crash; if that was all, it would've been enough. But no, then there were the cat creatures and the wolves. Not to mention Michael, poor Michael; he had seemed like a nice guy. Forced to do what he did for EnGen, but then forced to do what he did for Neola, out of love and maybe a little of wanting to do the right thing. And then finally, the car chase. I won't forget the car chase. I would have loved to have one of those wrecked sportscars.

Now we needed to try to destroy the records of Neola. *How were we going to do that? What would happen when we tried?* We were not soldiers. Besides, I'm sure they had the place securely guarded.

Exhausted, I slouched back in my chair, resting a while and thinking about the challenges that lay ahead. I think I started to doze because when the sliding glass door clicked open, I jumped.

Neola stepped out. The slight breeze blew her hair back and forth across her face. Her beauty was like nothing I had ever seen: so perfect, so angelic. I sat up from my slouch, transfixed on her face. Her skin was so smooth and white, her features just right. There wasn't a thing out of place, nothing to distract from her beauty.

She looked down at me while closing the door. She smiled as she caught my eyes, "Hi," she said.

"Hey," I said as I nonchalantly nodded at her.

"I'm sorry, were you asleep?"

"I may have dozed off for second."

"Do you want me to leave so you can rest?"

"No," I said nearly cutting her off. "Please, sit down," and I directed her to the chair beside me, not wanting to sound too eager and trying to play it cool. Luckily, she sat.

We stared out at the park for a few quiet moments before Neola broke the silence.

"I'm sorry I put your family in danger," she said as a tear rolled down her cheek.

"Oh, don't be. We chose this the moment we let you and Michael step onto the plane with us," I said, placing my hand on her arm as it rested on her chair.

"That was because of a lie. Your family didn't know the truth about me, about Michael."

"Yeah, but we still would have crashed the airplane in that area, and if we didn't have you with us to help with those creatures we would have all been dead," I reminded her. "You saved us. It's the least we can do."

"But there's likely more danger ahead. I have no clue about how we're going to get into the building, locate the files, destroy them, and still get out safely."

"Let me and my dad worry about that. You just focus on improving your skills. We will likely need them."

"I will," she said, still a little saddened.

"Hey, can I ask you a question? But if you don't want to talk about it yet, I will understand."

"Sure, what is it?"

"When we were on the gravel road, just before Michael was shot, you screamed, "Look out." Did you see the guy with the gun down the road? I didn't see you looking that way. The sound of the shot came after, so it wasn't like you heard it, did you?"

"No I didn't hear the shot or see the shooter. I felt it coming. I knew the bullet was on its way before the guy pulled the trigger. I don't know how else to explain it."

"Have you done that before?" I asked.

"Yeah, but only for little things. Like when the nurse knocked the glass off the table, I knew it was going to happen even before she hit it. I turned and told her to watch out for that, but before I could finish my sentence, she knocked it off. It is a weird feeling, but I can just sense something bad is going to happen, but it has never been soon enough to prevent it. With all these abilities, I can't stop the bad things from happening. It's worthless if I can't help people."

"But you have; you are," I reminded her once again, but it didn't seem to be enough for her. She still thought she should have been able to save Michael. "There's a limit to everything. You're special and have many abilities, but saving someone who's been shot just isn't one of those. You can't be so hard on yourself for that. I'm sorry about Michael, but you can't beat yourself up over it. He knew what he was getting into when he took you away from that place. It was a risk he was willing to take. He obviously thought you were worth it."

"Well, I didn't ask him to!" she cried, stood up and ran into the park. I had gotten up to follow her when the sliding glass door opened.

"Brad," Dad called to me. I stopped and looked back at him. "Yeah?"

"Don't go too far. In fact, please stay within sight of the motel. We don't know if or when EnGen's people will find us."

"I know," I snapped at him and continued after Neola.

She was in the middle of the park, leaning against a picnic table when I reached her. I took her hands in mine and gently shook them. "Hey," I said softly. She looked at me with her tear-filled eyes. Using my finger, I wiped the tears off her cheek as I said, "it's going to be OK."

She stared at me for a couple of seconds and then, without warning, kissed me square on the lips. I pulled away, separating our lips, and looked into her eyes. I couldn't resist! They drew me back in. I let our lips touch once again. She was everything I'd hoped for, everything I wanted. She was kind, thoughtful, and beautiful. She was so different from other girls.

We kissed for what seemed like minutes. She let go of my hands, reached up and wrapped her arms around my neck, embracing me tight. I placed my hands on her hips; so soft and so warm. The taste of her lips kept me there wanting more.

When we did finally let loose our kiss, she held her embrace and looked at me with passion in her eyes. There was a sense of longing in her, a sense of belonging.

"Hi," I said smiling at her. It was all I could think of at the time, taken aback by the kiss.

"Hi," she said back to me.

"You feeling better?"

"Yeah," she answered and then hugged me. We embraced tightly, her warm body against mine. The sun was setting and the park was beginning to darken. I wanted to stay right there holding her. I didn't want to let go.

Looking over my shoulder, she asked, "What's that?"

"What?" I said as I turned around to see what she was looking at. I was a little saddened because our embrace began to separate. "What, the swing set right there?"

"Sure, what is it for?"

"Really?" I said in amazement. "Come on." I took her by the hand and led her toward the playground. I playfully started to run, still holding her hand. She did the same. We reached the swing. It was an older standard metal pole set with seats attached to a long chain hooked to the top bar.

"Turn around and sit down, OK?" I said to her. She's scooted herself back into the seat and grabbed a hold of the chain on each side of her. I bent down and stole another quick kiss. I then got behind her and began to push her, slowly at first, then higher and higher until it was as high as I could get her to swing. I grabbed her swing as she came back and took off running forward with her. I pushed her hard as I went under her, letting her go. She screamed with excitement and fear. She giggled as schoolgirl would at recess. I watched her with amazement and couldn't help smiling the whole time. She started to slow down.

"You have to pump yourself to keep going," I said. "Here, let me show you." I went to the swing beside her, grabbed the chain, made a run for it, and jumped on. "Now, as we go back, you sit up and lean forward like this. When we go forward, you stretch out and lean back as far as you feel comfortable doing. Lean forward, lean back, with each swing."

"Like this?" she asked.

"There you go, yes. But if you keep doing it that hard, you'll continue to climb and when you reach a certain point, your swing will want to sort of continue around the pole. But your weight will not let it, and your swing will hop, or jump a little, and scare you," I said.

"So you're saying I'm fat?" she said playfully.

"Hardly!"

Swinging higher and higher, she let out a little scream when her swing finally did jump as she started forward. "Like that?" she asked giggling.

"Exactly!" I said. "Be careful."

"This is fun," she exclaimed. "It makes my stomach feel funny."

"That's why it's so much fun. The harder you swing, the funnier your stomach will feel, especially leaning back some and closing your eyes."

We must have swung for 30 minutes before Dad called us in. "We'll be right there," I called back.

"How do you stop this thing?" she asked, laughing.

"One of two ways," I said. "You can drag your feet every time you swing back, or you can jump." I exclaimed as I let go of the swing and allowed my weight to carry me off the swing at near-perfect timing. I stuck my landing with both feet square on the ground. "Tuck your arms in against your body so the chains don't catch on them, and then let go before you reach the top of the forward swing. You want to sort of glide out forward, not up. Now you try."

A little nervous, she swung back and forth gaining the

courage she needed, then let go. She flew forward, hitting the ground and stumbling a few steps as I helped to catch her. She stood up laughing, which slowed to a chuckle, then just a smile as she looked up and our eyes met. I pulled her close one more time and kissed her.

"We'd better go," she said as she motioned toward the rooms.

"But I don't want to!" I playfully whined.

"We'll have more time soon."

"Oh, all right," I said playfully. We held hands as we walked back.

"I had fun," she said. "I loved the swing." She giggled.

"I had fun, too. See you in the morning," I said and put my hands on her cheek and ear as I pulled her in for one more kiss. She hugged me, squeezing tight before letting go. We both watched the other as we entered our rooms.

"Good night," she said.

"Good night," I said. We closed and locked the doors.

# CHAPTER 20

**I brushed my teeth and put on shorts and a T-shirt. All** I could think about was Neola, her kiss, her smile, her laugh, and oh yeah, her kiss. She was someone I could get used to being around.

"We need to talk about these files on Neola," Dad said, snapping me out of my daydream.

"What do you mean?" I asked. "About destroying them?"

"Well, maybe. We need to decide if we should risk everything for this girl. They're not just going to hand them over. We'll have to take them by force. To destroy them won't be easy, and maybe even impossible, not to mention dangerous. It would also put us directly in the hands of those we're running from."

"I realize that, but with her help, we can do it. I know it! We can't just turn our backs on her now," I pleaded.

"I'm not saying that. We just need to weigh the options. Maybe it would be best if we take her away from this place, somewhere far away," Dad said.

"Like where?" I asked. "They'll find her. They have the money and the people to do it. Especially if they feel she is valuable, or dangerous to them."

"I don't know. A new start for all of us would be good. They're looking for me as well, because of what I know," Dad said.

"But where? Great Britain?" I asked.

"Maybe," Dad answered.

"Can't we try first, and then if we can't, then we can disappear?" I pleaded. "She will always be looking over her shoulder. We know how that feels. Would you want her to feel that way for the rest of her life?"

"No. I know that wouldn't be a good life, but realistically there's no other option. I mean, how do we do it? Do you have a plan? Any ideas?"

"I don't know," I snapped at him. "Maybe we just walk up to the front door and have Neola just tell everyone to go do something else."

"That could work, but what if they have a jamming system at that place like their cars had, then what?"

"I never thought about that," I said.

"I hear you, Son and I want to help her out as well. But we just can't walk in to this blind, without a backup plan for the backup plan. Lives are at stake here. I'll tell you what, let's think this through. If we can come up with a decent plan, then we will do it. But if we cannot, we must give it up and disappear," Dad said. Just remember, ultimately, we'll have to get your mother's approval."

"OK," I answered. We sat and discussed options from going in guns blazing, to kidnapping an employee, brainwashing them, and having them destroy the records for us. Each plan only hurt or killed other people, innocent people who just happen to work for EnGen. Just because people worked for that place doesn't mean they should suffer or die for it, as Michael and Dr. Gibbs had, or even Dad's friend and copilot.

In the end, we decided it was best for everyone involved to disappear. Neola had enough money to make that possible. The only thing that bothered me was that Michael was adamant Neola destroy the records of her existence. *Why? Just so she didn't have to look over her shoulder? So she would be safe? So she could have a somewhat normal life? Or was there some other reason he didn't have a chance to tell her?* Whatever the reason, he gave his life for this girl.

*If there was another reason, what was it? Maybe as simple as her being one-of-a-kind, or maybe because the company didn't know how to re-create her or someone like her. Could they figure it out if they had her? Study her, or cut her open to discover how she works?* Horrible thoughts ran through my head as I lay on my bed. I feared for Neola. She was on my mind as I started to drift off and was out cold within minutes.

All at once, I was standing in a vast open space, disoriented. *How did I get here?* I looked around. There was a hospital bed in the middle of the large room. Bright lights were shining down on the bed, which lit up the area as bright as day, causing me to squint. Surrounding the bed was darkness. Standing on the fringe of that darkness were people looking on.

Three people, two men and one woman were standing over the bed. All three were wearing scrubs and doing something to the patient. There was no movement from the person under the cover on the bed, likely knocked out for the procedure.

The doctors worked with such vigor and determination. It was clear they had to succeed. I saw a scalpel in one surgeon's hand, and a type of pliers in the assisting surgeon's hand. The nurse was using a suction device to keep the area clear for the other two. I looked back at the people in the darkness, most with their arms crossed over their chest, supervising the procedure. One was wearing a high-ranking military uniform, as if they were forcing the doctors to keep going. With the darkness of the area, combined with their focus on the procedure, no one had a clue I was standing there.

Curious about what was going on, and with having a strong sense that something was wrong, I slowly walked forward. The feelings in my heart forced me to go see who it was on the bed, caring nothing for my own safety. Staring at the bed, glowing from the bright lights, I inched forward. My heart was pounding.

I felt a tickle on my cheek as I stared at the bed. I wiped my face, tears? I was crying! A frantic sense of sadness overwhelmed me. Scared as to who I would find, I inched forward still focused on the head of the bed.

One surgeon was working feverishly near the head of the patient, blocking my view of the person lying there. Standing directly behind the surgeon with the scalpel, I wept, still not quite sure why. He paused, realizing I was standing there. He turned around and looked at me, as if angry with me for interrupting his procedure. Blood covered his green surgical gloves. Light glistened off the exposed stainless steel of his blade.

As if proud of his work, he pulled down his mask and smiled at me as he stepped aside to show off his masterpiece. I looked from his uncompassionate, dark eyes down to the person lying on the table. It was Neola. With the top of her skull cut off and her brain exposed, the other surgeon prodded it. I could tell he, too, was smiling behind his surgical mask. He looked at me, as did the nurse.

I screamed as I looked at her, obviously dead. Laughter erupted from the small crowd of people watching the procedure. "Get him!" the officer said pointing at me. A couple of others started toward me. I panicked, but before I could run, I awoke.

I sat up fast. A little disoriented, I didn't recognize where I was. In the darkness, it all seemed unfamiliar. After a few moments, and waking up a little more, I realized I was in bed in the motel room. It was only a dream. A sense of relief came over me. I looked over at Dad, sound asleep. The glowing red light of the clock's display read 4:15 AM. I lay back down and stared out the small exposed section of the sliding glass door into the darkness of the park.

I thought about the dream and how sad I felt. My heart hurt and my eyes were wet from crying in my sleep. It was a feeling I didn't like. She looked so awful lying there on the table, so exposed and so gone.

I was wide awake now. There was no way I was going back to sleep. I continued to stare out into the darkness of the night thinking about everything. *What was that?* I saw movement outside. I panicked. *Did they find us?* I jumped up, ran to the glass door and peeked out of the curtain. At first, I saw nothing, but then about 10 feet away and heading into the park walked Neola. She was dressed and had her bag over her shoulder.

I quickly pulled on my jeans, put on my shoes, grabbed my sweatshirt and went back to the door. Slowly but quietly I slid the door open and slipped through. Carefully I closed the door and took off after her.

"Neola," I whispered as I approached. She jumped around, startled.

"What are you doing?" she asked me.

"I was going to ask you the same thing."

"I'm leaving," she said with tears in her eyes. "I must get as far away from you and your family as I possibly can. I would just die if something happened to any of you because of me."

"But you don't have to leave us," I said. "Dad and I talked, and we're going to take you away from all of this and disappear to Great Britain or someplace far away. He knows people there who can help us."

"I can't; I must destroy those records just as Michael said."

"Why? What is the urgency?"

"Because!" she snapped. "Since they don't have all the files after Dr. Gibbs destroyed most of them, they can't continue the research without me. I'm not safe. I will never be."

"But that doesn't make sense. Even if you destroy the remaining files, they can still get you and start over."

"No. Right now, with me they can re-create the destroyed information because they have the other half of the research. If I destroy those files, even if they had me, they cannot re-create all the research. Does that make sense? With me and half the research, they are complete, but with me and no research they are not."

"Yes, I understand. Those files contain enough information to be the other half of the research."

"Exactly, but it gets worse," Neola said. "For them to be able to re-create the missing files, they will have to operate on me. They will have to cut into my brain, and I may not survive that."

"But can't they just 3-D scan it like Michael talked about?"

"Yes, I guess they can get a lot of data from that, but they will likely have to cut into me for the real data. Maybe they will do it just because of my rebellion. Maybe they will just start over."

"Now I understand their determination. I'm so sorry. Maybe that's why..." I stopped.

"What?" she asked.

"Nothing, nevermind," I said, thinking about my dream and why I had it. Maybe she was subconsciously communicating with me her worries while we both slept. *Why else would I have that dream?* "So it seems you have to destroy the records." I said changing the conversation back to what we were talking about previously.

"I must destroy the records even if I die trying. I'm dead anyway, as long as they exist," she continued.

"Well, I'm going with you." I said.

"No! I must do this on my own."

"Sorry, but I can't do that." I said as I grabbed her waist, pulled her close to me, and looked into her eyes. "I care too much about you now. Where you go, I go."

"But if something happened to you, I wouldn't be able to live with myself," she said, staring back at me.

"Nothing will happen," I said and gently kissed her lips. "Now wait here. I want to leave a note for Mom and Dad."

I ran back to the room and quietly sneaked in. I found the motel's tablet and pen and wrote:

> Dad and Mom,
> Neola and I went out for a little while. We'll be back soon, so please stay here and don't try to find us. We will be OK. I will explain everything later. I love you, Brad.

I quietly grabbed some food, picked up my backpack, and sneaked back out the door. I took Neola's hand and said, "Let's do this." She looked at me for a second then turned and we walked away.

# CHAPTER 21

**It was a warm, dry night. I held Neola's hand as we** walked. We were silent. We knew this was going to be difficult, even dangerous, but I don't think either of us knew what to expect. Something about her made me want to risk my life for her. *Could I really have fallen for her over the past day or so? Or am I just intrigued by her, by what she could do?* I hoped it wasn't the latter.

Crossing the park, we came to a road. We headed back into town, hoping we could find a bus or a cab.

"I dreamed about you," Neola said breaking the silence. "That's why I was leaving." She paused as we continued to walk. I didn't say anything; just let her collect her thoughts. She continued, "I dreamt you died, Brad! But it wasn't just a dream. It was so strong I felt it was a premonition. There was smoke and fire in the background. I figured the farther away from you I got, the less likely it would happen."

"It was just a dream Neola. That's all. I care about you. I felt something the first time we caught each other's glance. I had a dream about you too. They caught you and cut into you. It was awful." I said as I stopped and faced her. "Don't you see we both had one? I don't have your abilities, so how could I have a premonition. It was just a dream. We both had dreams and nothing more." She gave me a hug, wrapping her arms around me so tight I couldn't breathe for second.

"I don't know how, but you have a way of saying just the right thing at the right time to make me feel better. For the first time, I feel safe," she said as she let go of me.

"Thank you." I gasped and smiled. "So what are we going to do?" I asked as we started again toward the lights of downtown.

"I don't know," she answered. "Probably make someone take us to the lab where the records are kept."

"But what if they have a signal-jamming system like the car's had? Then what?"

"I will have to hurt people. I don't want to, but I will. This must stop. They killed Michael."

"How?" I asked.

"Move things into them, manipulate them. I don't know."

"Can you pick up things that big?"

"I think so, but I don't know yet how big. When I get mad or scared, I can do even more. I proved that when they were testing what I could do before Michael and I left."

"You know where to go?" I asked.

"Yes, I'm going home." She answered.

"Back to where they held you? Why?"

"After Michael and I left, they moved all the files and lab books back to try and re-engineer another person like me," she said.

"How do you know that?"

"I'm not sure, I just do. There's a cab, come on," she said just as I was about to ask her to explain more about how she knew that.

We ran to the next block where we intercepted the cab before it turned. The driver stopped and we climbed in.

"You know where EnGen headquarters is?" I asked.

"Yes," the driver said.

"Please take us there," I said.

"Why would you want to go there?" the driver asked.

"Sorry, but that's our business," I replied.

"I would love to, but cannot."

"Why?" Neola asked.

"That's on the other side of the wall. I'm only allowed to stay on this side of the wall. I cannot transport to the other side. The law requires proper identification to travel to the other side. The regulations won't allow cab companies to do it, but I'll take you as far as I can," the driver said and sped off.

"What does that mean? Why can't you take us all the way there?" Neola asked him.

"You two not from around here?" he asked.

"No," Neola lied.

I knew, but I let the driver explain.

"Well, years ago, rich business owners got tired of their homes and businesses being broken into and robbed. With their money and influence, they were able to force local government to segregate what they called their side of town with the lower-class side of town, which was everyone else. They paid to build the wall. Now to get across, one has to have permission or a reason. Not just anyone can cross. If you work there, they allow you to cross, with specific identification. If you were born on that side within the past 20 years, they genetically altered you to have a specific gene that would allow you to cross any time you wanted. It has something to do with your vision and being able to see different colors. Similar to when a person is colorblind, they can't see all the colors, but usually only shades of gray. When a person has this gene, they're not colorblind, and they can see another shade of the primary colors yellow, red and blue. There are systems that can scan for it in your blood, but the easiest test is a vision test. They have you look into a device that randomly generates a code in a specific color. If you have the gene, you can see the color and the code. With that gene, they allow you to do things not everyone can do, like use the low-cost transportation system. To ensure unauthorized people don't attempt to get across the wall, they increased security. If you try, they will throw you in jail for a minimum of a year."

"Wow," was all Neola could say.

We sat quietly for a while, holding each other's hands. I fiddled with her fingers. Her hands were soft and warm.

"I'm nervous," Neola said to me.

"Me too," I replied taking her other hand. "We'll be OK, you'll see."

"I sure hope so. Sometimes I wish I could just disappear and not worry about all this, but I know I can't."

"That would be nice. Hey, by the way, how do you

know they moved the records back? Did Michael find out and tell you?"

"No, I just saw it. It was as if it was an actual memory or something. That's best way I can explain it."

I looked up and saw the driver was watching us in the rearview mirror. He looked away when he saw me looking at him. I touched Neola on the leg and placed my finger over my lips as I pointed to the driver. She got the hint to watch what she says.

We drove for about 10 minutes in silence, looking at each other and watching the lights of the buildings flash by. As we exited the parkway, I knew we must be close.

"You know, if it wasn't for the same businessmen I would be out of a job," the cab driver said, breaking the silence. "They helped to create the Inner City Transportation Act a few years back requiring that not all forms of transportation be automated—some must have a human driver or controller. This was to ensure employment for many; otherwise, these cabs would have been robotic. There's no real need for human drivers."

"Well, that's one good thing they've done," I said.

"Yes, yes it is," the driver said.

"We will take the tram to EnGen. We should be there in about 15 minutes," I said quietly to Neola, staring into her eyes.

"OK, that sounds good," she said.

"Excuse me," the cab driver interrupted. "I don't mean to eavesdrop, but the tram doesn't start running again until 7:00 AM. You'll have to take the orbs"

Neola saw the worry in my eyes when I looked at her.

"What?" she asked. "What's wrong? What is the orbs?"

"I'll explain later," I said.

After a few minutes, we arrived. We got out and Neola retina-scanned payment to the cabbie, who then drove off.

"What is the orbs?" Neola asked, not wasting any time. "You look so scared when he said it, and I want to know what it is."

"Well, it's the Oregon Rapid Bulb System that transports one person at a time in a bubble to their destination on the other side of the wall. We call it the orbs"

"A bubble?" she asked.

"Yes. It starts as a glowing light. You step up to a mark, and when the light floats to you, you jump up about a foot and into the light. I heard the light appears halfway between the floor and the ceiling, out of nowhere. They're light blue, but with sparks and flickers as if electrified. The light then descends, floating down toward you. When it gets close, it will turn yellow. Then just as the light is a few feet above you, it will turn red. This is when you're supposed to put your arms up and into the orb. As you touch it, you jump. From what I understood, once you're not touching the floor, the light changes, pulling you up and centering on your body. The light grows based on your size, and surrounds your whole body.

Once it covers your body, it hardens into a bubble. It is kind of like a force field, enclosing you inside. You can stand or sit, but it makes a glowing oval shape around you, and you float up. Once outside the building, it takes off fast and you fly along a path to your destination. There are rings you pass through every so often that propel you along or turn you around corners."

"I guess I'll have to see it to believe it, but it doesn't sound too bad," she said.

I looked at her. "But there's a problem."

"What?"

"Not everyone can see the orbs. And I'm one of those who cannot. There's something about a specific genetic flaw, or as the cab driver explained, the lack of a certain gene. If you don't have this gene, you can't see the lights, so you can't use the system. If you can't see the light, you don't know when to jump into the bubble. There are rumors out there that say if you don't have the gene, you won't stay in the bubble and will fall out to your death. Others say that's just something they say to stop people from trying to use it, to stop the non-purists from using their system. That's what they call people from this side of the wall. But it's been said that people have tricked the system before. If one can time the jump just right and concentrate real hard, they can use it. They can escape to the other side for a better life."

"I wonder how they chose what gene to make work with the system?" Neola asked.

"It's one that's genetically altered when the baby is still in the womb. They've been using this gene for years for other things as well. Mom didn't do it on any of us because there were rumors of side effects, and of fetal deaths. Some say it causes mutations, or that babies can be born dead. But others say it is a scare tactic used by the rich to stop those from this side of the wall from using it."

"That sounds awful," Neola said looking at me concerned. "So what do we do? I wonder if I can see the light?"

"You know, I don't think I will fall out if I get in the bubble. I think that's a misconception. And I'm sure they put the gene in you, especially with you being from that side of the wall. So what if you go in first and pay, if you don't mind, and lead me. Then I will get in front of you. When it's my turn, and it's time for me to jump, you'll signal me with a cough or something. When you do, I will jump."

"But what if that doesn't work? What if I tell you to jump too soon or too late? They will arrest you won't they?" Neola said nervously.

"It will work; I trust you. You'll know when to tell me to jump because the light will change from yellow to red. The moment it changes red, you cough. As for if it doesn't work and I get caught, you'll do your mind trick thing on them, and tell them to let me go," I said, smiling at her. She smiled back nervously. "It will be all right, you'll see. Come on. Now after you pay, let's act like we don't know each other. That way, no one will get suspicious when you cough. You'll let me go ahead of you because you'll be nervous. Tell me you're nervous when we're close to the orbs, so the guards will hear you."

"OK, let's go," she said bravely and we headed up the cement steps to the main entrance. We walked up to the ticket counter.

"Two please, to the west-side station," Neola said to the woman behind the glass window.

"That will be one hundred and twenty credits," she said. Neola placed her thumb onto the sensor and the light turned yellow. "Give these to the agent at the loading station," she said, handing Neola two orange slips of paper.

"Thank you," Neola said.

We walked to the line that led to the orbs. Even this late at night, 50 or 60 people were ahead of us, with more coming in behind.

"I can see them," Neola said, seemingly to herself, but letting me know she could see the orbs.

"Great!" I whispered.

I stood in line behind Neola. All I could see was her long flowing blond hair. Even from my position, I could tell she was beautiful. When she looked around, I would catch a glimpse of her face. She looked different from the side. Her fair complexion and strong features made her a person I wanted to stare at; I noticed many men in line were compelled to do the same. I imagined many would see her baby blue eyes and be unable to look away.

The line moved forward slowly, or at least it felt that way. When I was about the 10th person in line, I became even more nervous and looked around to try to get my mind off the orbs. The building resembled an old-fashioned airport where people used to pile into airplanes by the hundreds and fly to their destinations. It was so dangerous, and I was told every so often one would crash, exploding from the fuel they used, killing everyone on board. With this new travel system, no human life had been lost, other than the rumors of those trying to cheat the system. This orbs station was only an inner-city transportation system. There were orbs for traveling city to city and yet others for crossing state lines, which were stationed at the larger transport building near the edge of the city.

The lighting above us was dim to look at, but strangely bright. People moved back and forth, hustling to get into line. Looking ahead, I saw the next person in line ready to go. She was standing at the counter with the attendant handing the ticket to her and touching the screen, selecting the info for her destination. The attendant scanned the card and said in a monotone voice, "Step forward to the mark on the floor. When the light turns red, look up at it and jump with your arms up in the air. Thank you for using O.R.B.S Travel." It was obvious she repeated the same thing over and over.

The woman stepped forward, looked up as if at the ceiling. After a few seconds, she put her arms up, jumped about a foot off the floor, and started floating up.

Once the light engulfed her, it turned clear and hardened into a plastic-looking bubble. Then the bubble floated up and exited a hole in the building. Once the bubble lifted off, it accelerated to speeds approaching 200 mph as it traveled to its destination. I'd heard international travel bubbles hit speeds of 400 mph. That was where the rumors came from. People say if a person did not have the special genetic trait and tried to fake it, at such high speeds, the force pushed the person out through the bubble's wall. But that didn't make sense to me because once the bubble hardened, the person couldn't push through it, so why would a person fall out? I sure hoped it wasn't true!

I continued to watch people check in, step up to the mark, jump into the air and float away. I could see the bubble after it hardened around them; I just couldn't see the light. Watching the people around me, a man just ahead of Neola seemed very nervous. He was looking around, looking at the attendant and then at the guards. He also seemed to be counting to himself, as if timing the lights. He nervously handed the attendant his ticket. The attendant asked him if he was OK. "Yes," he said. "I don't like to travel, but I have to."

"Step forward to the mark on the floor. When the light turns red, look up at it and jump with your arms in the air. Thank you for using O.R.B.S. Travel," the attendant instructed.

"Thank you," the man said as he stepped away from the counter to the small red dot on the floor, just as a person ahead of him floated away. He seemed to really be focusing, but not on the bubble. After a few seconds, he stuck his arms up and jumped. He came back down, both feet square on the floor, obviously missing the bubble.

"Guards!" the attendant yelled and two armed men ran over to him. They each grabbed an arm and said, "Come with us!"

"No, I just jumped at the wrong time," the man pleaded. "I'm just nervous. I don't like these things."

"You missed the light completely," one of the guards said. "In fact, there wasn't even a light. It was turned off temporarily because the attendant suspected something was up."

"You know it is a federal crime to attempt travel?" the other guard said as they walked the struggling man off the floor and through the security doors. "It is for your own safety," I heard the guard say just as the door slammed behind them.

Neola turned around and looked at me scared.

"It will be OK," I mouthed to her. I, too, was nervous but knew I wouldn't show it as that man had. I was sure I would be fine because I had her to help me with the timing.

The line started to move again. Neola was third in line now, and I was right behind her. She looked back at me again.

"Hi, are you nervous?" I asked her, playing as if I didn't know her, one guard standing only a few feet away from us.

"Yes. This is my first time," she answered.

"Would you like me to go first and show you?"

"Sure, you would do that for me?"

"Anything for a beautiful girl like you," I said playing with her again, trying to ease her mind. We switched places in line and I only had one person ahead of me, who was standing at the attendance's counter.

The attendant handed back the man's ticket and he stepped up to the mark. I was watching him, focusing on how he prepared for the light. I didn't hear the attendant the first time.

"Young man, step up, please," she said again.

"Oh, sorry," I said as I stepped forward and handed her my ticket. "I was just thinking about the man the guards took out of here. What will happen to him?"

"Likely jail time. Now, step forward to the mark on the floor. When the light turns red, look up at it and jump with your arms in the air. Thank you for using O.R.B.S. Travel," she said.

"Thank you," I said as I took the ticket back and put it in my pocket. I looked back at Neola. "Have a good flight," I said, smiling.

"Thank you," she said.

"Miss, please step up," the attendant said to her. Distracted by the attendant, I worried for a moment whether she was going to be able to signal me properly; to time the light just right, but without warning, she coughed. I immediately put my arms up into the air, looked up and jumped, probably a little higher than I needed to.

It seemed as if time slowed. I close my eyes and waited, hoping the bubble would grab me. *Please grab me. Please grab me,* I thought. It hadn't yet, and gravity started to pull me back down to the floor. A rush of panic came over me. *Oh no, I missed.* Just as I thought my feet were going to make contact with the floor, I felt a sense of weightlessness, and my feet never touched the hard tile. It was the strangest feeling I had ever experienced. My stomach was going crazy. It was 10 times greater than the sensation of driving fast over a small hill in the road.

As I floated away, I looked down at Neola and instantly worried about her, leaving her behind. She was stepping up to the mark as I entered hole in the wall. I waved at her. She gave me a quick but nervous wave back. I was sure everything was going to be fine, but I could no longer see her because I was through the hole and outside. *Please be OK, Neola.*

I turned around facing forward and looked down. I was already about 30 feet above the building and floating higher by the second. In no time at all, I was at least 200 feet off the ground. I'm glad I wasn't afraid of heights. There was a beeping sound inside the bubble, and before I could locate the source and figure out what it was, I accelerated at lightning speed. The force of the acceleration pushed me back, I rested against the transparent bubble. I felt as though I was going to push through it and fall out.

After a few seconds, my body became used to the speed and I could move around once again. Still concerned about the bubble, I pushed on it behind me. It felt very solid, so I knew I wasn't going to fall out. The rumors about people without the specific gene falling out of the bubble as it accelerated to max speed were just that, rumors.

I was finally able to relax and enjoy the ride. It was so much fun. Better than any amusement park ride. The buildings I flew past were a blur. I couldn't really make anything out. One building would blur into the next, making weird shapes for my eyes to interpret. I started to feel queasy, so I looked straight ahead. That, too, was a rush as buildings ahead approached with such speed. At first, it appeared I was heading straight for them, but as I got closer I would turn and fly right past.

Every so often, I would approach large rings. As I passed through them, I would feel a small burst of speed. Others appeared staged closer together. I would enter one ring and slightly turn before entering the next. Five to 10 rings lined a corner, depending upon the sharpness of the turn.

After only about three minutes, I started to descend and then slow down. It was over. I'd made it. The bubble slowed to almost a hover as I approached my destination. I continued down and eventually passed through another hole in the wall. As I got close to the floor, the beeping started again. After about five beeps, and only a few feet above the floor, the bubble disappeared, letting me go. I dropped to the floor and landed squarely on my feet. *What a rush.*

I looked around and saw people ahead of me walking through a roped-off area and toward the exit. I slowly followed, looking back for Neola. After a couple seconds, a bubble appeared through the hole in the wall, and I smiled in relief.

The bubble released her, and she stumbled only slightly before catching herself and walking my way. She had the biggest smile on her face.

"Wow! That was fun," she said to me and gave me a big hug. I picked her up and swung her around, playing with her. We both were amped up after our ride. I gently sat her feet back down and looked at her. I was glad to see her and relieved that leaving her behind didn't end badly. I would never have forgiven myself.

Still staring into her eyes, I saw her smile fade, and she reached up and pressed her lips against mine. She closed her eyes, and I looked at her for a second before I closed mine. Her smell, her taste, I was falling for her, fast and hard.

"All right, all right, move it along." We stopped kissing and looked up. A guard was standing a few feet from us. He motioned to the exit, but before we moved, he smiled. It was nice to know not every guard was all business. It showed they were people, too.

I let my embrace go, grabbed her hand, and we walked out. We were happy in the moment, and each step felt as though we were still floating as we moved through the double doors and stepped out onto the sidewalk. We hadn't a care in the world, swinging arms as we held hands.

Once on the sidewalk we looked left, then right. It was then that reality started to hit us; the joy each of us had from our recent ride left us. The gravity of our situation came across our faces and we were quickly back on task.

"A taxi?" I asked her.

"Yeah," she answered. I walked over to a row of taxicabs and opened the back door of the first one. I looked back at Neola, expecting her to be right behind me. She wasn't. She was walking away, down the sidewalk.

"Neola," I called to her, trying not to yell. She didn't acknowledge me. I looked at the cabdriver, said I was sorry, and shut the door.

As I walked toward her, she stopped next to a man sitting on the sidewalk who appeared to be homeless. She bent down.

"Excuse me," Neola asked. "Is your name Ben?"

"Yes, how did you know that?" he asked.

"I just see things sometimes, and felt I needed to talk to you."

"Why would you need to talk to me?"

"I'm not sure yet," Neola said, placing her hand on his arm.

He just stared at her. His dirty face and long unkempt beard surrounded his tired eyes. He looked sad as he studied her. I'm sure he was wondering who this girl was.

"You have a son," Neola continued.

"Yes," the man said to her, a little puzzled.

"His name is Jacob."

"How do you know?"

"And you haven't talked to him for seven years now," Neola added, ignoring him. He didn't respond.

"You had a fight, about your wife, his mother. She passed away, I'm sorry."

His eyes started to gloss over as he continued to look up at her. He never said a word as she continued to tell him facts she felt about him.

"Your son blamed you for her death because of the accident. You were driving when the car hit black ice and spun out of control, crashing into a tree. The car struck the tree on the passenger side. She died later that evening."

By now, tears were flowing down the man's face. They washed away any dirt they encountered, leaving clean streaks down both cheeks. He wiped his face with his sleeves.

"Jacob was twelve. He loved his mother so much. She was an extraordinary woman. Losing her crushed the both of us, and any chance of a normal relationship between the two of us. Her death was hard.

Our car had one of the early generation self-driving systems, but I didn't like nor trust it. So I never used it.

164

The crash was avoidable, according to the police report, if I had the car in auto drive. Because of that, Jacob blamed me." The man paused, tears flowing strong. "We fought until he finished high school and moved out. I was not motivated after that. I walked away from everything. I have been living on the streets ever since."

"Well, he should be about 24 years old, right?" Neola I asked him.

After a long pause, he said, "yes."

"He's married and has a son of his own," Neola said.

"What?" the man asked.

"It's true. Your grandson will be four years old tomorrow. Jacob wants his son to know you, and you to know him. Jacob is looking for you, and has been for about a year now. You should go see him. Would you like that?"

"Yes," the man cried.

"Here, give me that," Neola said and took his electronic credit machine. People could securely transfer money by way of the machine with just a thumbprint. Neola entered the number of credits she wanted to transfer to him and approved the transaction with her thumbprint. She handed it back to him.

The man looked at the screen. It must have been a lot, because he appeared shocked when he read the numbers.

"Now, here is his address, she said as she tore a piece of cardboard from a box next to him. Using a marker he had for his sign, she wrote Jacob's address for him. Take those credits, find a place to stay and get yourself cleaned up. Your grandson is waiting for you, and you want to make a great impression, right?"

"Yes, thank you so much," he said to her.

"You're welcome," she said and gave him a hug.

"What is your name, miss?"

"Neola."

"God bless you, Neola. I will never forget you." Neola smiled at him as she stood back up. She looked at me and said, "I thought you were going to get a cab."

"I... But...," I stuttered.

"Gotcha!" she said and poked me in the side. I flinched and laughed.

"That was pretty cool, what you did for him."

"I was just glad I could help."

"EnGen, please," I said to the driver as I opened the door of the cab and we climbed in.

"They're closed this early, are you sure?" the driver asked.

"Yes, we're going someplace close to there, but don't remember the name," I answered, bending the truth to stop the questions.

"Oh, OK," he said and drove off.

Neola was still holding my hand. She squeezed it and looked at me more nervous than ever. The cab pulled away from the curb. We headed down the street. There was a thick, clear plastic wall between the back seat and the driver. Only a few small holes drilled in it to allow sound through. Below the plastic, centered in front of us, was a touch screen. If we wanted to, we could access our bank, surf the Internet, or even watch a show. It was also where we paid when we reached our destination.

"You OK?" I whispered.

In a soft, quite voice, she told me, "I think so. It's been awhile since I've been there. I'm just scared to go back, afraid they'll lock me up again. I don't want any more tests or experiments. I just want a normal life."

"Can I ask why you didn't leave before, try to escape?" I looked up at the driver to see if he was still watching us. He was looking at the road.

"I didn't know anything else. My whole life I only remember being there. Where would I have gone? What would I have done? Now I know what is out here. I know people like you and see there's a better life than in that lab. I don't want to go back. I just can't." Tears started to run down her face. I caught one with my finger and wiped it off.

"You won't get stuck there. I will do what I can to make sure that doesn't happen."

"I know you will. I just worry the two of us won't be able to do anything against them. It may be like before, where they have a jamming system that didn't allow me to control them. Then we will be stuck."

"Well then, the first thing we will have to do is take out that system. We have an advantage. They won't expect you to walk in the front door. They'll likely have it off. But if they don't, we will figure out how to make someone show us where it is and we'll destroy it. Then we can move on to the records," I whispered to her.

"Here we are," the driver said.

# CHAPTER 22

**Slowing down as we approached EnGen, I looked out** the window. Off to the left was a huge campus of various-sized buildings, each lit up with its own set of security lights surrounding them, exposing every possible shadow.

"Where would you like to be dropped off," the driver asked.

"Pull over right here," I said.

We stopped at the vacant lot adjacent to EnGen. A barbed-wire fence surrounded the facility, with the only way in being the gate in the front of the facility. A guard station stood next to the gate.

Neola paid, touching the thumb pad on the touch screen. The doors popped open. We got out on the same side and the cab drove off. There we were staring at the place that had imprisoned Neola for the past 16 years. Now she was back facing her captives. I could only guess how she felt and what was going through her mind. She was trembling.

"Come here," I said and pulled her in. I held her close "Are you going to be OK? You still want to go through with this?"

"Yes, I must or, or Dr. Brandt died for nothing," she

stuttered. "I must, and they must pay. I noticed she wasn't trembling anymore. She stepped away from me, pulled herself together and said, "Let's go."

We walked on the sidewalk toward the guard station. Inside the fence, patrolling the perimeter, were men with drones hovering about 30 feet in the air above each of them, and spread out around the facility. Each drone had spotlights that shone along the fence, quickly highlighting any dark areas then turning off a few seconds later.

The sun wasn't quite beginning to rise yet, but a hint it wouldn't be long was evident on the horizon. We approached the shack. A lone guard sat behind the glass window. He spotted us right off and slid the window open. Before we could even say anything, he said, "Hey, you're that missing girl!" He started to reach for his video radio.

"Yes, but you're not going to tell anyone," Neola instructed him.

"No, I'm not," he said.

"You'll call a guard out to escort us around, but don't tell him or anyone else who I am."

"OK," he said and picked up his handheld video radio. "Johnny, are you still in the lobby?"

Johnny's face appeared on the small screen. "Yes, what's up?" Johnny responded.

"I need you out at the shack. I need you to escort some visitors."

"This early? It's not even 6:00 AM yet. Who is it? Show me." The guard looked up from the handheld video screen to Neola who shook her head no.

"Just get out here!" he said and shut the radio off and

put it in his back pocket.

We waited for the second guard to arrive. Neola told the guard in the shack to come outside. As he approached us, we saw he was sweating. I wondered if he was aware of what was going on but couldn't do anything about it. Maybe this was why he was sweating. He did look nervous.

She told him Johnny, the guard coming out, was going to be busy for a while, and to make sure no one called him for help for the next couple of hours. We thought that would be plenty of time. Then she told him we were someone else, high-level management's relatives here for a tour. She told him he wasn't to alert anyone of their true identity.

After a couple of minutes, the second guard, Johnny, drove up to the shack in a small personnel cart. We turned our backs to him so he didn't recognize Neola until he was close enough for her to control him. As he stopped, Neola turned around and told him to relax and to take us to the lab. He looked at the other guard, who was standing next to the shack looking apprehensive, then back at us as we got in the cart. Without question he drove off, taking us toward the building. I looked at Neola. She sensed my staring and looked over at me. She forced a smile and looked back at the building. I could tell she was nervous.

The sun was approaching the horizon, causing a bright red glow to ignite the dark eastern sky. The cart stopped and we got out.

"First take us to the device that prevents me from controlling everyone," she ordered to Johnny.

"Follow me," Johnny said.

We walked through the main doors and into the lobby. It was a large reception area with windows on three sides. On the back wall was a guard's desk, likely where Johnny sat, as nobody was sitting there. To the left of the desk was a door with a sign on it that read, Authorized Personnel Only. To our right, a long hallway led into the depths of the building. At the start of the hallway was a pair of elevators.

We walked past the desk and started down the hall. As we entered the hallway, I noticed a door across and elevators marked security.

"Is anyone in here?" I asked Johnny.

He looked at Neola. She gave him a look. "Yes. Bob is in there monitoring the cameras and drones."

"And he is alone?" I continued.

"Yes. Normally there are a couple of guards stationed in there, but since it is the weekend, we only have one.

I looked over at Neola. "We need to make sure he doesn't let anyone know we're here," I said to her.

Neola looked at the guard. "Open it!"

Johnny put his thumb on the pad on the wall and the door clicked. He turned the handle and went in. Neola stepped in behind him and immediately ordered the other guard to turn off all recordings and not call or let anyone know she was there. "Did you notify anyone I was here?"

"No, I didn't recognize you," he answered.

"Go about your business as if it was a normal, quiet Saturday," she said to him. "OK, let's go," she said to Johnny and me.

We left the security room and continued down the hall.

It was dark and eerie, with only half the lights on. After a few corners, we stopped at a door labeled control room. Then Johnny placed his thumb on the pad and the door clicked. He opened it and we went inside. The room was empty of any personnel and filled with various equipment and computers. Some were running and some were not.

"This is it here," Johnny said, pointing to the strange generator-type machine, not running.

I bent down and started pulling on wires. Some were hard to break. "Do you have anything to cut with, scissors, pliers, or a knife?" I asked the guard.

Looking at Neola first, as if for permission to speak, "There should be some scissors in the desk," he responded as he turned to face the desk. He opened the drawer, pulled out the scissors, and handed them to me.

I proceeded to cut wires everywhere I could, removing entire sections of wiring so someone couldn't easily reconnect them. I then cut the power plug. It was thick and very hard using the scissors. Satisfied there wasn't much else I could do to disable it, I said, "That should do it. That should slow them down."

"Now, take us to where they have all the records and data on me, all the lab notes and journals."

"This way," he said and led us out of the room. We went around a few more corners, through some doors, farther into the building. There was no way I would remember how to get back. I knew we would have to find another way out of the building unless Neola remembered the way back.

We came to a laboratory the size of a warehouse. It was

a sterile-looking room with cabinets and stainless steel countertops down one side. The center of the room was filled with large cylinders extending from the floor up about 6 to 8-feet tall. The center portion of the cylinders was made of thick glass. They were filled with a murky liquid. Four rows of cylinders with at least 10 cylinders per row packed the room. It was hard to see the cylinders with only a few small lights glowing here and there.

"Where's the light switch?" Neola asked the guard.

"Over there," he said pointing to the left of the door we'd just entered.

"Turn them on, please," she politely ordered.

"But the records aren't here. We just need to go through this room."

"Turn the lights on!"

He walked over and flipped the switches on. One at a time, lights began to shine, starting closest to us and working their way to the other end of the room. The last switch he flipped turned on the lights within the cylinders. The light reflecting inside the liquid gave each cylinder a light green glow. The cylinder's lights also revealed most of them had something inside, floating. We slowly moved forward, following the guard across room, walking between two rows of cylinders.

"What is this place?" I asked Neola.

"I don't know. I've never been in here."

As we approached the first few tanks, we saw deformed babies connected by tubes and wires floated inside. Their heads connected directly to their shoulders. Their bodies didn't appear to have necks, and they had small stubs for arms and legs.

"What is that?" Neola asked stopping in front of one tank.

"I don't know," I responded, puzzled. "What is that sticking out of its back? Is that a tail?"

Protruding out of the baby's lower back, just above its bottom, was a deformed limb about a foot long, kinked to one side near the end. It started thick near the body and thinned toward the tip. The thing just lay there lifeless.

Staring at it for a while, we noticed our guide, Johnny, was still heading across the lab. We glanced at each other and then back at the thing in the tank before we moved on.

Each tank had a similar "thing" inside it. As we progressed across the floor, the things in the tanks seem to become larger than the previous one, with fewer deformities. The things were different. Some resembled humans; some were unrecognizable. One thing in common was they had no hair and appeared to have human skin as well as human facial features. Freaked out, both Neola and I didn't like walking past them, especially on both sides of us. Neola drew close to me as we walked.

We approached the last few tanks. Finally, we were almost out of this place. The last tank in the row on my left caught my attention. There was something familiar about the thing in the tank. I stopped as Neola continued to follow the guard. She stopped at the door with Johnny and looked back at me.

I stared at the thing. It looked like a normal human. It was a female, fully grown. She had no hair, no eyebrows, and was very strange to look at. I slowly inched forward. *What was familiar?* I was only inches away from the tank. We were face-to-face. She didn't move, but just seemed to float there. I couldn't see her whole face because there was a breathing mask over her nose and mouth. She had tubes stuck in her arms and legs that led down and into the floor of the tank. I stared at her face. She had her eyes closed and appeared dead. There were no bubbles coming from the mask, and her chest didn't appear to be moving so it didn't seem to me she was breathing.

"Let's go!" Neola said.

"Coming," I answered and looked at Neola. Then it hit me. The girl in the tank looked like Neola. *Were they close to cloning her?* I looked back at the girl's face, then at Neola.

"Neola, I hate to say it but she looks like...," I started to say. All of a sudden, the girl's eyes popped open. Still, only inches from the tank and close to her face, it scared me. I jumped back, falling against the tank behind me. Catching myself I stood up and found myself face-to-face with another girl, very similar to the other one. She, too, opened her eyes. Once again, I jumped, stumbling as I headed over toward Neola and the guard. "They're alive!" I gasped. "They opened their eyes."

"I know. I can hear them," she said.

Neola took a few steps forward, toward the tanks. She stood there for a few moments. She yelled stop and covered her ears, as if trying not to hear some horrible, loud sound. A sound only she could hear. I ran over to her.

"Are you OK?"

"No! I can't get them out of my head!" She screamed as tears welled up in her eyes. "They're crying and asking me to help. I don't know what to do. I need to get out of here!"

"This way," the guard directed, and he walked through the door.

I put my arms around Neola, helping her, and I followed him out. Just before the door closed, I looked back at the girls in the tanks. I will never get those images out of my mind. I turned and we continued down another hall toward the door at the end. I held her close as we walked on.

# CHAPTER 23

**Through the door, we found ourselves in a very large** laboratory. There were tables spread throughout the lab. Computer systems were set up on some of them, while others had microscopes and other test equipment. To the back of the lab was a large glass room.

"That's where I lived," Neola said, pointing. "I was allowed out of it only when they conducted experiments on me, testing what I could do."

"That sucks," I said walking over to it. "It's not very big."

Looking in to the glass room, I saw a bed in one corner with a small table next to it. Two chairs sat in front of a display unit where she could probably watch programs or maybe even someone communicating with her via the video system. There was one area in the back right corner of the walls not made of glass.

"Is that area the restroom?" I asked her.

"Yes."

"Well, at least you had some privacy there."

"I have so many memories here. I'm just glad I'm not stuck in there anymore. It was awful. There was always someone watching, writing things down. I had a nurse assigned to stay with me at nights when I was younger, but every time I would get close to them and start to get to know them better, they would be gone and a new one would come. Looking back, I think it was so I wouldn't get too attached.

"Sorry," was my only response I could think of. I didn't know what to say. It seemed so awful for someone to have to grow up in there. "Well, at least when we destroy the records, you won't have to worry about going back in."

"Destroy the records?" Johnny asked.

Neola turned to him. "Where are all the lab notes and records on me?" she asked, demanding he answer her.

"They're in Dr. Atkins's lab in the next room," he quickly answered, unable to control himself.

"OK, you'll wait right here for us to come back. Don't tell anybody about us, or the records we plan to destroy. Just sit there and wait. If anyone calls on the radio and asks what you're doing, you tell them you're still busy with the visitors."

Like a child given instructions by his parents, Johnny walked over to the chair and sat down. He looked a little lost and confused, probably struggling in his mind as to why he was listening to this girl. It was against everything he knew and was trained to do. But he sat there staring off at the lab's floor.

Neola and I walked to Dr. Atkins' lab through the door. It was a smaller room, with fewer workbenches. It seemed more specialized, having only certain types of test equipment.

"Do that to me," I said as we were looking around the

room for the records.

"Do what?" Neola asked.

"Control me."

"What? Why?"

"So I can see what it's like. Then I can tell you what it's like."

"I don't want to," she said, turning away.

"Come on, please?" I begged her playfully. "Wouldn't you like to know what someone feels when you take over their mind? Do they know you're in there? Do they fight it? I could tell you; I would like to know myself."

"Well, I don't know," she said.

"Please, please, please," I said as he got down on both knees in front of her begging. My silly attempt at a sad look made her laugh.

"You're pathetic," she said smiling. "OK, you asked for it!"

Before I could even get up, she said, "If you're going to beg, you have to do it the right way, on your hands and knees."

Without hesitation, I dropped down placing my hands onto the floor.

"That's it. Now wag your tail, as if you had one," she said laughing. I began to swing my butt side to side. I felt silly but couldn't stop. "You're tired and thirsty, stick your tongue out and pant." I complied.

"Stop wagging and beg on your hind legs only," she ordered. I put my hands up in the air and sat on my back legs as if I were a dog begging at the dinner table, hoping for scraps. "Stop begging, roll over on your back and submit." I did as she ordered, putting my hands and feet slightly up in the air as a rollover on my back. "That's a good boy," she said, squatting down and starting to tickle my belly.

She stopped tickling me instantly, and released my mind. Seemingly embarrassed, she stood up a little red in the face, and composed herself.

"That was so cool!" I said, standing up and dusting myself off. "I was fully aware of everything, but no matter how bad I didn't want to do it, I had to, as if my life depended on it. It was the strangest feeling."

She was a little distant. She wouldn't look me in the eye. "Is everything OK?" I asked her, smiling.

"Yes," she said. "We should keep looking so we can get out of here."

Neola and I wandered around for the next few minutes. Very cluttered, the laboratory had stuff everywhere. It seemed disorganized, as if someone wasn't sure what they were doing. This was going to take a while. I looked over at Neola. She was staring at the wall, lost in deep thought.

"Are you sure everything is all right?" I asked her.

"Being back here, I don't like it, but it also feels like home. I'm very torn. Part of me wants to stay, because it's all I've ever known. On the other hand, I despise what they're doing here. I hate them for that and want to get as far away as possible."

"Yeah, I can't imagine what this is like for you. I remember moving once when I was younger, having to leave my friends, school and my home, everything I knew, to move to Portland. It was hard. I didn't want to leave. It was all I knew at the time. But now I would never want to move away. Yeah, we could do with less rain, but otherwise it's great here. I have my friends, school, boxing, and my family. Things change, life changes. We have to adjust and go on."

"Wait, boxing?" Neola asked. "You box? Isn't that fighting? I saw it once on one of the channels they let me watch. It looked pretty rough."

"Yeah, I've been boxing for years. I enjoy it."

"I didn't know that about you."

"Yep, it's just something I do. That and baseball. So, what was it like the day you left here?" I asked her as I picked up a stack of papers to see if they were about Neola or the testing going on here. Even though we should be rushing, I felt so relaxed in her presence.

"It was normal for me that day. We were doing the bullet-deflection tests when Michael came in and stopped it. He was mad about something. I later found out that it was because they were shifting my training toward me becoming an assassin or something like that. They'd already taught me some self-defense moves, and with the bullet-deflection tests they were performing, he just blew up. He was so mad that their mission had changed from helping people with Amyotrophic Lateral Sclerosis and other neurological disorders, to a military application, he decided it was enough. Both he and Dr. Gibbs were finished with Mr. Roberts and what he had them doing to me.

Michael took me straight to the back exit and we walked right out. I asked him many times where we were going as we made our way to his car. He just told me to hush and he would explain later. We were out of the gate before anyone knew what had happened. We just kept driving. It wasn't until we were at the old airbase and the hangar he broke into where Michael finally told me why we left. He had no real plan, just to try to get as far from EnGen as he could. I was scared. I'd never been out of the lab. Everything was so big."

"Oh man, that must've been hard for you," I said. "Your whole life, everything you knew was gone in one day."

"Yes. Michael was so glad your family came along. He said he had no real idea of what to do to protect me, but he was going to do everything he could to try," Neola said as she started to tear up.

"Come here," I said as I stepped up to her and pulled her in close. "I'm really sorry about Michael. He seemed like a good guy who cared about you."

Neola didn't say anything. She just stayed there in my arms crying. I squeezed her tight as she sobbed. I think she was finally able to grieve for him. Everything had happened so fast since he died, there was just no time. But she needed to get it out so that she'd be able to move on; at least that's what I'd learned in my psychology class. I was glad she was finally able to cry and I was there to help.

We stood there for what seemed like minutes until she slowly lifted her head from my shoulder. Wiping the tears from her eyes, she apologized as she tried to compose herself.

"No, don't be sorry," I said, nearly cutting her off. "There's nothing to be sorry about. This is normal. You have done nothing wrong, and it was not your fault. Do you hear? Never allow yourself to think that. They did it! It is their fault! They did that to Michael and we're going to make sure nothing like that happens again. Let's find these records and destroy them."

I moved back deeper into the lab. Over near the back, a stack of boxes full of papers and notebooks lay across a table.

"Is this what we're looking for?" I asked as I walked over to some boxes. I picked up a notebook and thumbed through it. Neola came up beside me and began looking through a few notebooks.

"I think so."

"Well, how do we really know? And, how do we destroy them?" I asked.

"Destroy what?" A voice came from behind us.

# CHAPTER 24

**Startled, we jumped and spun around.** There was a short man standing in the middle of the room looking at us, a cup of coffee in one hand and a file folder in the other. He was balding and wore glasses. What hair he did have on the side of his head was sticking out in every direction. He wore tan slacks. His collared shirt, exposed by the unbuttoned white lab coat he was wearing, was partially untucked. It looked like he hadn't left this place for a week.

"Who are you?" I asked.

"I was about to ask the two of you the same, but now that you have turned around: Neola, how are you?"

"Better than ever, Dr. Atkins," she responded.

"You know him?" I asked.

"Yes, he was one of the many scientists working with me, on me, or whatever you might call it."

"I'm surprised to see you back. You're the last person I expected to walk into my lab. And who might you be?" he asked, looking at me.

"A friend!" I said, somewhat snobbishly like.

"So you have a friend," Dr. Atkins continued. "This is good. What else have you been up to these past few days?"

"They killed Dr. Brandt," she said.

"I know, I heard. I was saddened when I found out. I didn't feel that was necessary."

"Necessary?" Neola cut him off raising her voice and the lights started to flicker. "What about moral or ethical? Who gives them the right?"

"Now just relax," Dr. Atkins said in a soft voice, looking up at the lights. "I agree that they didn't have the right to do what they did, but I can't tell them that. Now, did I hear something about destroying records?" He asked, trying to get her mind off of Michael.

"Are these the lab notes and papers on me and this project?" Neola asked him.

"Well, no. They're for a project I'm working on."

"Did you forget I can read your mind? They are the records! We're going to destroy them. Are there any more?"

"No," his voice said, but his mind betrayed him.

"Brad, over there is a box and a few on the desk," she said, pointing behind the doctor.

"No, you can't do this!"

"We can, and will!" Neola said.

"Neola, just come back. We'll take care of you, you need us."

"Need you? Ha!" she said. "I know what you have been doing here is wrong. I see there's a real life for me out there. I want no part of this any longer and plan to ensure you and any other scientist can't continue the work Dr. Brandt and Dr. Gibbs sacrificed themselves to protect. We're destroying everything."

"Neola, there will be someone else who will take up the project. You won't stop them."

"Well, then, I will slow them down."

"And maybe we report to the news and the authorities what's going on here," I said as I carried the box of papers and sat them down with the rest.

"Those things in the other room; some are alive, "Neola said. "Isn't that right? That's how I was made, isn't it?" she yelled. Tears trickled down her cheeks.

"Neola, I'm sorry," Dr. Atkins said.

"Enough talk!" she said and appeared to take over his mind. "This is all the records?"

"Yes, with these," he said and handed her a folder and a flash drive he had behind his back.

"What about the computer?" she demanded.

"There's a file directory on you, and your financial records."

"Can you delete them?"

"Yes."

"From here?"

"Yes."

"Well then, do it."

He walked over to the computer. With the movement of his hands in the air, as if pushing things around that weren't physically there, the virtual display populated with Neola's picture and other data.

"Delete it all!" she ordered. He paused as if fighting her. "Do it! Delete it!" she ordered. One by one, the information was deleted until everything was gone, pictures and all. "Now, what did you mean finances?"

"They're tracking your finances. They know everyplace you use them."

"What? They are? Who?" Neola said, looking at me.

"The company," he said.

"Did they track yesterday?"

"Yes. In fact, I was surprised to see you here without them. That's why I'm in here this morning. I was expecting them to capture you at the motel and bring you back in."

"No!" I exclaimed. "Mom, Dad and my brothers; we have to go back!"

"OK, we will," she said to me. "Can you stop the track on my finances?" she continued directing the question to the doctor.

"No. I don't know how."

"Is there anybody here who can?"

"No, not this morning."

"We gotta go. What chemical here will burn hot and fast, before the system can put it out," I asked.

"That stuff there," he said pointing to a blue five-gallon jug under one of the lab benches.

"Help us!" she ordered the doctor. "Get the chemical and bring it over to the files. Brad, get the computer while I get the files off his desk."

We went to work. We piled up all the books, papers, computer and the flash drive. Neola instructed the doctor to pour the whole five gallons of chemicals onto the pile.

"Do you have any matches or a lighter?" I asked the doctor.

"There's a striker over there on the lab bench, but I don't think you want to use that. You'll need to stand way back when you light it because it will ignite fast."

"What do we do?" I asked.

"Wait, everyone stand back," Neola said. "Over by the door," she pointed.

The doctor and I backed up, making our way to the door. I was about to ask Neola what her plan was when I saw her put her hands over her ears as if blocking out all noise. She was staring hard, concentrating on the small mountain we had created. All of a sudden, it ignited in flames that came out of nowhere. I looked at the fire, then back at her in amazement.

"Did you know you could do that?" I asked Neola when she came toward the doctor and me.

"Yes, I will explain later. Let's get out of here. We must get to your family. Dr. Atkins, lead us out fast and cover for us if anyone stops us."

"Follow me," he said as we exited the lab. The fire did spread quickly, just as he had said. I looked back and saw the plastic case of the computer melting. It was a hot fire.

"Faster," Neola said to the doctor. "You! Go back to the front desk, quickly," she said to the guard sitting right where we'd left him. "And don't do anything to stop us!"

We made our way back through the room where the engineered girls were and whatever else was in the liquid tubes. I was glad to be out of there. Through a couple more doors, and down a hallway, we had yet to run into any guards. But, no sooner than I'd thought that, Dr. Atkins ran smack into a guard as he rounded the corner.

"Are you OK, sir?" the guard said to him. "I'm sorry. I didn't see you."

Dr. Atkins looked at Neola and me before answering; a worried look was in his eyes. "Yes, I'm OK," he finally said.

His reaction, and the presence of the two of us, must have made the guard suspicious, because he narrowed his eyes as he looked at Neola and me before asking the doctor, "What's the rush, and who are these two with you? I didn't know about any visitors."

"This is my niece and her friend. I was showing them the lab for a school project but need to get them back to the front lobby and out before Mr. Roberts gets back. That's why we were rushing."

"Today, of all days?" he said, staring at Neola. "Where are their visitor's badges?"

"Oh, we must've left them in the lab. I will return them to the front desk later. I need to get these kids out."

Neola and I stood watching. One call on the radio to the other guards and the way out for us would become much harder. The doctor handled himself well, and it appeared the guard believed him. *Thank goodness,* I thought. *The quicker we get out of here, the better!*

"You know the rules about visitors." He paused in thought. "OK, but return the badges today."

"I will, thank you."

We started off again. I followed Neola around the guard who stood in the hallway, staring us down as each of us passed. Just as we rounded the corner, the fire alarm went off. I heard over the guard's radio another callout, "There's a fire the west lab."

"Hold it!" the guard yelled as he rounded the corner, seeing us running. Neola stopped so suddenly, I nearly ran into her.

"We don't have time for this!" She turned around and told the guard to leave us alone and to go about his business. "Forget we were even here," she instructed.

Without hesitation, the guard put his gun back into its holster, turned around and disappeared around the corner. I looked at Neola and smiled. We took off again.

"Why didn't you just tell him to leave when he first got there?" I asked her as we moved down the hall.

She told me, "I don't like to control people if I don't have to. I was hoping the doctor could get him to leave."

We weaved around the hallways of the large facility for what seemed like forever. We must be almost out. Sure enough, the last corner and finally the lobby was just ahead. As we were quickly making our way down the last stretch of hallway, two guards wearing strange looking helmets walked from the lobby and stepped into sight.

"They're on to us," Neola said. "I can't control them while they have those helmets on. They must be blocking me somehow."

"Slowly walk toward us," one guard said as the two of them held some kind of rifle pointed at us.

"What do we do?" I asked her. "We can't run back because they will shoot us before we make it around the corner," I continued, looking behind us at the long hallway we'd just come down.

We were just across from the security office, but if we made a break for it and the door was locked, they might start shooting.

"OK, we're coming," Neola said to them. She turned

around to me and mouthed, "Sorry."

We started walking toward the two armed guards, taking our time as we both were surely trying to think of something. Nothing was coming; no brilliant ideas.

"What if you start a fire on one of them?" I asked.

"I don't want to hurt them, and besides, what if they react by shooting? I don't want you to get hurt either," she said.

"Stop!" the guard ordered us. We were only 10 feet from him.

"Dr. Atkins, go stand over there, please, while we attend to these two," the second guard said to him, while pointing to the visitor's waiting area. "Mr. Roberts will be here shortly."

Neola looked at me, worried.

"All right, turn around," the guard said. Just as we were turning, the front door to the lobby opened. It was the guard from the shack out front. He, too, was packing a rifle, but he made one mistake; he wasn't wearing a helmet.

Neola looked at me and turned around as she winked. I turned around too. We both stood with our backs to the guards.

"Bind their hands," one guard said to the other. But before he took a step toward us, we heard a click from one of the guns behind us and knew the safety was off.

"Don't move! Slowly place the guns on the floor," a voice said.

Neola and I turned around. The young guard who'd entered the front door was standing behind the other two, pointing his rifle at them.

"You fool!" one of the guards yelled. "I said to stay back if you didn't have a helmet."

"Well, take yours off and join me then," Neola made the young guard say to the other two.

"No!" the guard said, whining, clearly torn as to what to do. The other guard started to reach for his helmet and then stopped, waiting for his partner to decide. "Damn it, Mike!"

"Then you'll die," the young man, who was obviously Mike, said as he stuck the barrel of the gun to the back of the guard's head and pushed on the helmet, letting him feel the proximity of the gun.

The other guard quickly pulled off his helmet, while the first hesitated. The gun resting against his helmet must've changed his mind because he finally gave in and took it off.

"All three of you, go help with the fire. Take your time getting there. Leave your guns here, and forget everything that has happened today, and forget you've seen us," Neola ordered them. "Wait," she continued as they started to walk off. "You, go to the security office and delete all video recordings from this morning and stop all recordings. I know you turned them back on. Now go!"

The two guards continued down the hall, while the third unlocked the security office door and entered it as instructed.

"Doctor, let's go," she said to Dr. Atkins, who stood in awe watching the whole thing. We left the lobby through the main doors and walked down the steps to the front parking lot. "Where's your car?" she asked him.

"Over there," he said, pointing to a silver Audi sitting in

reserved parking.

"Does everyone who works here have to drive an Audi? I asked. "What is the voice code to start it?"

He hesitated as if embarrassed. After a moment of pause, he leaned over and whispered it to me. I chuckled. "Really?" I stared at him. "OK Mama's boy, we're going to take it with us. You need to leave this place."

"Forget all your work on the Neola project, and any project similar to it," Neola said. "Go find a different job where you can use your talent and training to help people. Now go!"

He started to walk off toward the front gate, as Neola and I ran the rest of the way to his car. We jumped in, me in the driver's seat and Neola in the passengers. I pushed the power button and the access code light came on. "Mommy," I said, and the car came to life. Neola and I looked at each other and busted up laughing.

I backed out of a parking spot and started to drive away. Just then, there was a huge explosion, and I looked back through the rearview mirror. The west lab was ablaze, a plume of smoke and fire shot through the roof of the building and up into the air. Boy, were they going to be mad. Neola turned around in her seat with her knees on the leather as she watched the lab burn. She had a look in her eyes of relief and gladness.

We drove past Dr. Atkins, who was standing beside the guard shack, staring back at the fire. He seemed confused and lost. We shot past the guard shack and out onto the road, racing to get back to the motel.

# CHAPTER 25

As we drove farther from the laboratory, the size of the fire didn't seem to shrink as everything else did. It was growing so fast and had engulfed the complete building. Neola, now turned around forward in her seat, watched the road ahead. She seemed to be in deep thought. I didn't bother her, and we sat quietly as we drove back toward the motel. I'm sure the destruction of the lab, the place she grew up, the place she had known as home for so many years, bothered her. But knowing what that place really was, she must've felt some relief to be moving on. We drove for about 10 minutes with neither of us saying a word. Buildings streaked by as we sat in soothing silence.

"They're going to be pissed," I said, finally. "I just hope they don't take it out on my family."

"It will be OK," Neola responded. "They won't. They need us to cooperate and must be smart enough to know that if they hurt your family, the lab is only the first thing I will destroy."

"I hope you're right."

"I am," Neola said with a confident, caring smile as she put her hand on my arm. I stole a glance at her before I had to turn to watch the road again. I could have put the car in auto mode but wasn't quite ready to give up driving yet.

"How are we going to get back to the other side of town?" she asked. "Do we have to take the orbs again?"

"Are you reading my mind?" I asked, smiling.

"No. I would never," she said.

"I was just messing with you. I was thinking about the same thing. No, we don't have to use it again. Besides, faking the system once was lucky, doing it twice and on the same day would be nearly impossible. No, there's a bypass we can take."

"Why couldn't the taxi take it?"

"The taxi didn't have the software required, but this high-end car does. It's programmed to show the bridge on the map. Many older and cheaper cars do not have the software to see the markers required to follow the road. It's as if the road doesn't exist to them."

"Well, why can't you just drive in manual mode like you are now?"

"The authorities thought of that too. There are certain sections of the public highways that are off-limits to manual driving. They're considered too hazardous, or just not allowed. The bypass is one of those. The highway's monitoring system will just override the manual system and turn the car around. I hear there's a hefty fine for even attempting to take the bypass without the proper software or authorization."

"Do you know why they won't let just anyone move freely between the two sides of town?" Neola asked.

"Well, aren't you full of questions?" I kidded her.

"This is all new to me, remember?"

"I know. My dad says it has something to do with the rebellion. It was even right here in Portland, a big riot. That's why the black scorched area we saw was dark and totally destroyed, that's where it all happened. Certain leaders of the United States of America wanted to join the multination union that began in Europe. Well, some of the American people didn't want to. But the leaders were going to do it anyway. There was a big uprising, right here."

"But what does it matter if people go back and forth between the two sides?" Neola asked.

"Well, the center part of Portland was destroyed, never to be rebuilt, as a reminder of what will happen to the people and the homes of those who rebelled. They built the wall on the edge of it to separate the damage from the part of town where the major businesses are, and the housing development where the rich executives and politicians live. The working-class were the ones who started the rebellion, so most of them are not allowed on the other side, as punishment and social separation. They're filtered out by O.R.B.S, not allowed to cross unless it is for work. Most don't even attempt to cross anymore."

"That's sad," Neola said.

"That was a long time ago," I continued. "I think now the wealthy just feel they're better than everyone on the other side of the wall, and they don't want a certain class of people on their side of town unless it is to help them make more money and work in their factories."

"That's just weird to me."

"Besides natural birth, social status is another reason

not everybody has the specific gene to see the O.R.B.S."

"Like that other guy who tried to fake it?"

"Probably," I said.

I pulled over to the side of the road and searched the navigation system for the motel's address, selected it as the destination, and put the car in auto mode. Within a few minutes, we approached the bypass. As we entered the checkpoint, a green light turned on and the car continued along the road crossing the bridge. I breathed a sigh of relief as we put that section of town behind us. We were 40 minutes from the motel, according to the car's navigation system. The O.R.B.S. was much faster.

I was worried about my family, but talking to Neola helped keep my mind off them. I was especially worried about my dad. If they found out who he was and that he used to work for them, I didn't know what they would do to him. He feared for his life anyway, and with Neola in the picture, this was double the reason to take him out of the equation.

We drove in silence for most of the way, unfortunately for me. My mind was racing with all the bad things they might do to my family. The silence wasn't good for me. I also think shock was setting in about everything that went down at the lab, as well as what was likely waiting for us back at the motel. *What were we going to do?*

We exited the bypass, and the car continued on its route toward the motel. We were eight minutes away. It was pretty bright out, now midmorning. Time was flying by.

"You nervous?" I asked.

"Yes, you? Neola responded.

"Yep. What do we do when we get there?"

"I don't know, but I will help you get your family any way possible."

I thought for a moment about what they might be going through. *Were they being tortured? Were my brothers separated from Mom and Dad, and scared? Or worse, were they hurt?*

"Brad? Brad!" Neola said, raising her voice, snapping me out of my deep thought.

"Sorry, what?"

"We're here," she said, pointing to the motel.

"Oh, shoot!" I said as I fumbled with the car's controls to turn off the auto drive. If I left it on, it would drive us right up to the front door. Once off, I drove past the motel as we both looked around for anything out of the ordinary. Everything looked OK. There were no signs of anyone. I parked in the restaurant's empty parking lot next door.

"Let's go," I said.

"OK, but let's take it slow and not rush in."

"I have to help my family."

"I know, but we need to take it slow and see what we're up against. OK?"

I knew she was right, but I was thinking about what we might find. *What if they hurt my Dad and my brothers and just took Mom? Or hurt Mom and Dad and took my brothers? Or worse, killed them all.* I started to walk faster but Neola gently grabbed my wrist. "Brad!" she said quietly and took my hand.

"Yeah?" I asked, somewhat out of it.

"We need to be level-headed about this."

"Yes, I know, but we need to hurry."

"Brad!"

"Yes. OK, OK."

"I'm with you. We'll do this together. We will find them and they'll be fine."

I tried calming down. I focused, trying to control my breathing as Coach had taught me. I would just die if anything happened to them.

We walked to the front entrance. Looking around, we didn't see anyone suspicious outside. Slowly, we entered the main door of the lobby.

Peeking in, we didn't see anyone so we crept past the front desk. There was no one there. I walked up to the counter and looked into the office behind it. I could see nobody in the room. I looked at Neola, now right behind me. She shrugged.

"Let's go on," she whispered.

As we moved past the end of the counter, I spotted him. The manager was lying in a pool of blood on the floor behind the counter, half hidden behind the chair, dead. His eyes seemed to stare through us. I quickly looked at Neola, and after the fear took over, I started to run toward my parents' room.

Again, Neola grabbed my arm. "Wait. Slow," she said slowing me down. I couldn't concentrate. The fear for my family was unbearable. We cautiously went on, moving slowly down the dimly lit hallway. There were no unusual noises. It was quiet.

We made it to the corner and looked around. Nobody

was there, so we rounded it and moved toward the rooms. As we drew near, I noticed the doors to both rooms were standing half-open.

Neola and I traded glances, then crept on. As we approached the first room, where mom and my brothers slept, we peeked around the door. Nobody was inside. I went in to check it out and see if by chance someone was hiding in the bathroom. Again, nobody was there. But, their bags were still in the room.

I motioned to Neola to go to the other room, as I followed her out. Again, we peeked around the door to see if anyone was there. That room also appeared empty. There were clothes on the bed, and Dad's bag was still on the floor by the dresser. The bathroom was empty. They were gone.

"What now?" Neola asked.

"I don't know. We need to somehow find out where they have taken them," I said, looking around the room for any clues that might tell us where they were.

"I'm sorry for all of this," Neola said sitting on the bed. "This is exactly what I didn't want to happen."

"This is not your fault. We should've realized they were tracking your spending. That's how they always search for people running from the law. I guess we didn't realize just how powerful they were and that they could access your account."

"But if something happens to your family, I couldn't live with myself. None of you are part of this, and just because you helped me doesn't mean you should suffer. You didn't know what you were getting into." Tears were running down her face. One dripped from her cheek and clicked as it hit the floor. She looked down and noticed a piece of paper laying there between her feet. She bent down, picked it up, and stared blankly at it.

"We became part of it by choice," I assured her. "We wanted to help you. Once we found out who you and Dr. Brandt were, we could have separated ourselves, but we didn't. This is as much on us. Don't feel bad. Everything has a way of working itself out, that's what my grandmother always said."

"How? I don't...," Neola started then tapered off.

"What?" I asked.

"This paper. It is a note from them," she said in a surprised voice.

I sat down beside her on the bed and read the note. It was addressed to me:

> Brad, they're taking us to an empty warehouse on the Willamette River.

That was it, no other information or instructions.

"Do you know where that is?" Neola asked.

"It could be any place along the river, but might be where all the ships dock to load and unload cargo," I said. "But I don't know if we will be able to find exactly where they are."

"Should we go now and look?"

"I was thinking that, but we could spend all day looking and not find them. Let's pick up everyone's things and find a different place to figure this out, and then we will go find them," I said.

"OK. Do you know where you want to start to look?" Neola asked as she picked up a shirt off the bed and stuffed it into Dad's bag.

"No, but I need to think about a place they might be able to hide them without raising suspicion."

We picked up the rest of Dad's things. Just as we were finishing, I started to tell Neola we should head next door and pick up Mom's things too, but she shushed me.

"What? You hear something?" I whispered.

"Yes," she said, focusing hard. I couldn't hear a thing. We stood there for about a minute while I patiently waited.

"Well?"

"Someone is coming and I feel they're here for us. They're just passing through the lobby now."

"How do you know that?" I asked.

"I can hear them talking and I just know they're looking for us. They were left behind, told to keep an eye out for us."

"Should we hide?"

"No, I will make them talk, tell us where your family is."

"Where are they now? How many are there?"

"Almost here. They're in the hallway and there are only two."

We stood in the middle of the room waiting for them. I could hear them talking now that they were closer. Neola's hearing must be so much better if she heard them talking that far away. The voices were getting louder and louder by the second.

I was getting nervous. Neola must have been as well, because she grabbed my hand. I gave it a gentle squeeze to try to comfort her, but honestly, she comforted me. I didn't feel like I could really protect her. It was the other way around. This girl was amazing. The more time I was with her, the more amazing things I saw her do. Things I once thought were impossible.

As I stood in thought, the two men rounded the doorway talking. We caught them off guard, and Neola had control of them before they could even pull their pistols.

"Get in and close the door behind you!" Neola ordered, and they did as she said. "Put your guns on the floor." They obeyed. "Now, take a couple of steps back."

I walked over and took both pistols. With the fingerprint safety feature, the guns wouldn't fire for Neola or me, but at least they didn't have them. I would toss them out later. These two didn't seem like just security guards, but people who were willing to take it to the next level. *Were they planning to hurt us? Were they going to hurt my family? Did they already hurt my family?*

"We have to find out about my family," I blurted out.

"Where is his family?" Neola demanded.

"Taken away from here," one of them answered.

"Obviously! Are they hurt?" she asked.

"No, not really. The adult male was beaten up a bit."

"Who did it? Was it either of you?" I asked.

"No, it was another guy who's with them now."

"What is his name, and why did he hit my Dad?"

"His name is Frank. They were trying to get your

location out of him. He said he didn't know. After the explosion at the lab, they figured it was you and stopped questioning him," the man said.

"Where are they now?" I asked, but the man hesitated.

"They're in a warehouse," Neola said. "On the Willamette River, Port of Portland, pier 3. Wait, they're not at the port right now, are they?"

"No," the man said.

"You don't know where they are holding them, do you? Neither of you do."

"That's correct."

Neola stared at the two of them. After a long pause she said, "Well, give it to me, then!"

"What?" I asked as I saw one of the men take a piece of paper from his pocket. Neola snatched it from his hand. I walked over to her and we read the note together:

> If you ever want to see the boy's parents again, come to the Port of Portland, terminal two, but you already know that, don't you? The men will escort you there. Be there at six o'clock this evening. Don't take it out on my men; they're just doing their job.
>
> ~R

"Which warehouse is it?" Neola asked as she handed me the note.

"The largest one on the water's edge, the second warehouse you come to," the man said. "I heard the company owns it."

"What surprises will be waiting there for us?" she asked.

"We're not sure. They didn't tell us anything else about their plans, only the location. I think they knew you would get it out of us."

"OK, then you two are not of any more help to us. The both of you will forget that you talked to us, forget you saw us, and forget you helped us. Sit here and wait for us to arrive, as if we haven't yet. Do not come to the warehouse, even if ordered to. Just tell them you're going, but don't ever show up." Neola finished and looked over at me.

It still amazed me when she did that. Sometimes though, I still wondered if she'd ever done that to me and I just didn't remember. My heart trusted her, though my head was more hesitant.

"Oh, and one more thing," she said. "You'll never kill anyone again, either of you, unless it is self-defense of your own life or the life of your family, but even then only as a last resort. Now, we're going to get our stuff and leave. You two sit here until we come back or you're called back to the EnGen."

Neola and I took Dad's things and went to the door. Turning back to the two men who were looking forward in a dazed stare, we were satisfied. We closed the door.

We went next door to get Mom's and my brothers' things. As we were picking everything up, Neola caught me looking at her a couple of times. "What?" she asked.

"Nothing," I said, smiling. "I was just looking at you."

"Well, stop...,"

"OK. Hey, who is the person who signed the note, this

"R" person?

"He is the...," she cut her sentence off. "There's someone here!" she whispered.

I looked around in a panic. I worried more men were there and would shoot first, not allowing Neola time to control them. After we stood back to back in the bathroom doorway frozen for what seemed like minutes, I asked her, "How do you know?"

"I can sense them," she said.

"Who are they? How many?"

"I think there are two of them."

"Where are they? They aren't in this room; it's empty."

"I can't tell exactly yet, but they're close. Hold on, let me focus."

Neola stood there with her eyes closed concentrating on the threat of the men close by. After a few seconds, she opened her eyes and looked at me. She was smiling.

"What?" I asked.

"It's Parker and Zach. There under the bed."

The bed was a mattress on a wooden box frame. Its design didn't allow us to see under it. I ran over and lifted the mattress. There they were lying on the floor hidden and protected within the wooden frame.

"Brad!" they said in unison.

"Guys, you're safe!" I said, reaching to help them out, holding the mattress up with my other hand. "Get your backpacks."

After they were out, I lowered the mattress and grabbed them both, holding them tight. All three of us nearly wept.

"I'm so glad to see the two of you. How did you get in

there?"

"Mom put us in there when she heard them break into your room," Zach said.

"Yeah, and she said to stay there until you came back. We were scared you weren't going to come back," Parker added.

"So she knew I was gone?"

"Yes," they both said, looking up at me with tear-stained eyes.

"Well you guys did great," I said, trying to reassure them. "Now we have to get out of here. Ready Neola?" My brothers looked over at her as I said that, and after a second, they ran to her and gave her a hug. She looked at me and smiled.

"Ready," she said after they let her go.

We all headed out, cautiously walking down the hall and into the lobby. Before we came to the body, we had my brothers hide their eyes. We passed the manager and stepped through front door. "Wait, I have an idea. Stay here," I said.

I set the bag down, opened the zipper, and removed the two guns we'd taken from the men. I ran back inside and, using my shirt, wiped off the fingerprints. I placed the guns under the man's shirt, hiding them so only the police would find them. As I was getting up, I noticed his wallet sticking out of his back pocket. I pulled it out and found his ID. Looking at it, then at the man, I saw he didn't have a wedding band. His stare freaked me out. Slowly, I reached into his pocket and felt for his keys. I was sure he was going to snap to, reach up, and grab my hand at any moment. I quickly pulled my hand out of his pocket. With his wallet and keys, I went back out front. "Let's go."

# CHAPTER 26

**We pulled out of the parking lot.** I looked in the rearview mirror at my brothers in the back seat. I was so glad we'd found them and they were not with Mom and Dad. I just hoped they, too, were all right.

I saw Neola looking at me. She must've sensed my worry, because she put her hand on mine. "Everything is going to be OK," she said. "Your parents are fine, I just know it."

"You seem to have a way of knowing that sort of thing, but it's my parents, I can't help but worry. I hope you're right."

"Are you going to Chuck's house?" she asked, changing the subject.

"Who's Chuck?" I asked, confused.

"Let me see his wallet you have in your pocket," she said smiling.

I removed it and handed it to her. She opened it and took out his ID.

"Charles M. Thane," she read aloud. "The dead guy at the motel."

"Yep. He told me he wasn't going to need his place any longer, and we could hang out there this afternoon."

"Oh he did, did he?" she said, smiling at me.

I wish I didn't have to stare at the road right this second, because I loved her smile and would much prefer to stare at her. Even in the awful situation we were in, she calmed me. She completed me.

"Can you enter his address into the GPS so I can put the car in auto drive?"

"Sure," she said and typed Chuck's information into the computer on the touch screen. Once the car was in auto, I released the steering wheel and was able to relax. The display showed we would arrive at the house at 9:02 AM, 47 minutes from now. We'd spent so much time at the lab I was amazed we'd actually made it out of there. Realizing what had happened to Mom and Dad, I didn't like that they had been with these people so long, let alone the rest of the day.

I leaned my head back against the seat and looked over at Neola. She was still looking at the ID from Chuck's wallet. A tear rolled down her cheek.

"What's wrong?" I asked her.

"This guy didn't deserve to die. He was a good man."

"I agree he didn't need to die, but how do you know he was good? We only met him that one time when we checked in."

"I just know. I can see snippets of his life when I hold his ID. He was just trying to get by, just like everyone else. After his mom was diagnosed with multiple sclerosis and placed into a medical facility, he went back to school and was working part-time here to help pay for the classes. His dad ran out after his mom's diagnosis. Here's another family who could have been helped, as Michael would say, if EnGen had just continued the testing and research as they should have."

"You know that from just looking at his ID?" I asked in awe.

"No, from touching it. I see short stories, kind of. His mom gave him the house we're on our way to right now."

"Well, you continue to amaze me."

"It's crazy how I can do some of these things, but I'm realizing I sometimes don't like it. I don't like being able to know that much about a person, especially since I don't know them."

"Yeah, I imagine that would be weird. It'd probably make it harder for you to turn your back on someone in need, especially when you know and feel so much about them after just a brief contact."

Neola put the ID back in the wallet and handed it to me. I put it back in my pocket. She leaned her head back against the seat and just stared out the window.

As soon as I put the car in drive, Parker and Zach started talking at the exact same time. They were spewing their story, explaining every moment they were alone there. It was remarkable how they said almost the same thing at the same time. It must be a twin thing. I just let them tell me what they felt, saying a quick "uh, huh" and "really" every so often. When they seemed to be finished, I told them I was sorry they had to go through that, and I reassured them I wouldn't leave them alone again.

For the next 10 minutes or so, we all were quiet. We watched things pass by as the car took us to the house. I saw people walking down the street, going about their lives. There were kids playing in a small park without a care in the world. I wish my brothers could do that—be the kids they were and play carefree on a playground. I wish Mom and Dad once again could settle down and have a normal life, and for me to be able finish school and to work and start a life of my own, maybe someday. Maybe even with Neola, I thought, as I watched her looking out at the people we passed by.

"Approaching our destination," the car's voice said, breaking the silence and startling both Neola and I. We laughed at each other for jumping, as the car pulled up to the front of the house. "Shall I park at the curb here?" the car asked. The house was a small place with a tiny front yard and a driveway leading down the right side to a detached garage.

"No, I will take over," I said to the car.

"Releasing control now," the car said, and a warning beep sounded. I grabbed the wheel and took control. I slowly drove away from the front of the house and down the street to the next road. I turned right and saw an alleyway behind the houses. I turned onto it and drove to the back of Chuck's house. There was a gravel area behind the garage, so I pulled into it and stopped. It was just enough room to park and not stick out into the alley. I shut the car off.

"Did you happen to get a sense of anybody living with him?" I asked Neola.

"No, it seemed he lived alone."

"OK, let's go. Ready guys?" I said, looking into the back

seat at Zach and Parker. They were both staring out the back window. I don't think I remember the last time they were so quiet.

"Yep," they both said at same time. "Do you think Mom and Dad are dead?" Parker added, a tear starting to roll down his cheek.

"No buddy, they're not. They're just fine. Neola knows things and can tell they're OK. We will meet up with them later today, and everything is going to be the way it was soon. OK?"

"OK," he said.

We climbed out of the car and cautiously made our way toward the house. Crossing the lawn, we walked between the garage and in the house and headed up to the front door. I looked around the neighborhood, but didn't see anyone outside. I knocked on the door as a precaution, but after a few moments assumed no one was in there. I tried the keys and on the third attempt found the correct one.

Opening the door, I slowly entered. The house was quiet, and it appeared no one was there. My first impression was that for a single guy, the house was very clean and organized. It didn't seem as though he had taken much of his mom's things down because some of the items on the walls and tables were obviously hers.

I walked in the house, checking every room to ensure no one was there. We had the small, two-bedroom house to ourselves. My brothers ran over to the monitor screen and turned it on to see if they could find anything to watch. Immediately they found something and sat down, staring at the screen.

"Hungry?" I asked everyone.

"Yes, we're starved," my brothers said.

"I could eat something," Neola said.

"Well, let's see what we have," I said and went into the kitchen. Neola followed me. I opened the fridge as she sat on the stool at the kitchen counter facing me. I opened the meat drawer. There was an unopened package of turkey lunchmeat. "Now, let's see if we have some bread."

I opened the door that I thought was a pantry, and sure enough I was right. There was a loaf of bread on the shelf. I inspected it for mold. I didn't see anything and it felt fresh. I opened it up and smelled a piece. It was fine.

I went back to the fridge and looked for mayonnaise or mustard and anything else for a sandwich, like tomatoes, lettuce, pickles, and a little cheese. Neola was going to be impressed with this gourmet sandwich. I went to the drawer by the sink and opened it up. Just as I had hoped, it contained the knives.

"You know your way around," Neola said. "Are you sure you haven't been here before?" she laughed.

"This place is set up almost like our old house was. Anyway, there's just a kind of standard people use when putting things in a kitchen that make it easy to find."

"Well, I've never been in a kitchen. The food was always prepared for me."

"I don't know if that's a good thing or not. I like messing around in a kitchen sometimes. Well then, can I make you a turkey sandwich?" I asked.

"Yes."

"With mustard and mayonnaise, and maybe tomatoes?"

"Sure, sounds fine."

I made four sandwiches and sliced up some apples I found. I put them on plates and sat Neola's, and mine on the counter and took the other two to the boys watching their show. I came back in, made four glasses of ice water, and handed them out. I sat down beside Neola, who was already eating her sandwich.

"Well, how is it? Sorry it's not breakfast," I said, since it was only about 10 o'clock in the morning.

"Good," she said with a mouthful, but covering it with her hand. I smiled and took a bite of mine. The juice from the ripe tomatoes squished everywhere and dripped onto my plate. It was so good. It'd been a while since we'd eaten anything and didn't take long for us to finish. We didn't talk much while we ate. We were too busy inhaling our food.

"What are we going to do when we get there?" Neola asked.

"I don't know but think we should get there early to check things out. And maybe we can catch them off guard."

"Well, I'll do whatever I can, whatever it takes to free your parents."

"Thank you. I know you will. Hey, I know I've asked this before, but what else can you do? Abilities, I mean. I was just wondering what to expect or maybe to help plan our attack. Can you remember even the small tests they were doing with you that might be able to help us?"

"Let me see, I remember everything they tested," she said, then paused.

"Everything?" I cut in.

"Yes."

"Like photographic-memory everything?"

"Yes, that's what they called it."

"No way, really? I've always wished I had that ability."

"Remembering everything is not always a good thing," she said, sighing. "But, I do remember Dr. Brandt trying this one test on me where he had a match and he asked me to focus on the tip to try to heat it up, to light it."

"Did you light it? Is that how you were able to start the lab fire?"

"No, the match didn't light. But I did make smoke start to come off the tip."

"How many times did you try?"

"Just the one time. After the match test, we ran away. It wasn't an official test, though. He didn't record it, like the others anyway. It was just he and I that day, just playing around. He tested me with that, trying to create heat or fire. I tried it again in the lab, and that's how I started the fire. I also remember him testing me for precognition and premonition before that."

"What are those exactly?" I asked, cutting her off once again, so excited and interested in everything new I learned she could do.

She paused for a moment. "You know when Dr. Brandt was shot? And I screamed before it happened? Well I sort of felt or saw it happen before it actually did happen. I sort of felt the bullet coming. That's a form of precognition, consciously perceiving the future. Premonition is more subconsciously sensing future, maybe when I sleep or am very relaxed, or sometimes when I'm daydreaming. It is hard to explain."

"Pretty cool," I said. "Kind of like spidey-senses?"

"What?" she asked with a bewildered look on her face.

"I used to collect old comic books, the paper ones from almost a century ago. In one, there was this kid bitten by a specially engineered spider. It gave him powers and the ability to sort of see behind himself, to see something coming. You might say, to see danger just before it happened. Sort of like that?"

"Yeah, I guess," she said smiling at me.

"What else do you remember? Tests, I mean?"

With her finger pushed to her lip, she thought to herself, then said, "There was one test I thought was really fun. It was with a bow and arrow. They would shoot it and I would try to redirect the arrow. It was hard at first, but once I figured it out, it was fun. I could make the arrow hit almost anywhere I wanted to, in the same direction it was heading. I was getting better. They started having me try it with bullets, but that was much harder. The bullets were just too fast. Again, before I got really good at anything, we ran."

We lost track of time, engrossed in conversation. It was cool learning all about what she could do. As I sat there listening to her stories, I heard a horn honk outside. I went to the window and peeked out. I saw a little girl across the street playing outside with her doll and a stroller. The stroller was in the driveway. A man drove up in a new car. He stopped halfway up the driveway, just shy of the stroller. He got out just as Neola joined me at the window.

The small girl smiled and said, "Daddy!" She got up out of the grass and started to head his way, her doll in tow dragging behind her.

The man started to yell at her about the stroller blocking the driveway. The girl stopped in her tracks, halfway to him when her excited face changed and she instantly became sad, and scared. The man took the stroller and threw it into the yard. He got back in his car and pulled the rest of the way into the driveway.

"That poor little girl," Neola said.

"I know. He crushed her heart. She was so excited to see him and because of a bad day or something, he took it out on her."

"He is yelling at her about his precious car and to keep her toys off the driveway," Neola said.

"How do you know?"

"I can hear him. Can't you?"

"I wish I could. All I hear is his voice muffled, but his actions clearly tell me what the issue is. What a jerk!"

The man walked up the steps and into the house. The little girl stood there as if in shock, crying. I didn't like the way he treated her.

"How sad," Neola said as she turned from the window.

"I know. It looks like he loves that car more than he does the little girl."

"So, what were we talking about before that jerk interrupted?" I asked as we walked back over toward the kitchen counter.

"About my tests, but there wasn't really anything major, just moving things and controlling people, but you've seen that. Enough about me and my skills, what about you?"

"Me, well I don't have any kind of powers," I said sarcastically.

"You know what I mean," she said, bumping her hip into mine as we stood resting our arms on the counter.

"Me, there's not much to tell," I started then paused. She looked at me for more. "Well, my name is Brad," she chuckled then gave me a look, so I continued. "I'm seventeen. I played baseball in high school, before all this happened. I played left field. I box. I have been for years now. I'm pretty good at that. I love cars, especially sportscars. I really like the high-end cars, like the Audi, Porsche, and Ferrari, and hope to one day have one of my own."

"Well, you do—that car out back," Neola said.

"But I don't, it's not mine. It belongs to that scientist."

"He won't ever report it stolen. He doesn't even remember he owned it," she said.

"Well, that would suck. Did you completely wipe his brain?"

"No, I just told him to start over. He has his credits in the bank. He will go home, but anything to do with work at that place, well, let's just say he forgot all about it, even the car. When we were talking, I told him to forget about it. I had a feeling we were going to need it."

"I didn't hear you say that."

"That's because I didn't say it out loud."

"I can't keep it. It is just not right. And my dad wouldn't let me anyway."

"Well OK, but basically it could be yours. It is the least

they can do for you and your family. It was bought with the company's money; they paid him a car allowance while he was working there."

"What if his boss goes looking for him and asks why he is not going back to work and maybe finds out the car is missing and tracks it or something. They will find us."

"Maybe, but I doubt it. Dr. Atkins would just tell them he is through working there. After what he went through at the lab, and all his work being destroyed, it will seem there's nothing left for him to do anyway. They won't wonder about the car. It will be fine. If anyone does, I will tell them to not worry about it. That it is yours. And you know how I can make someone believe it." Neola said and winked at me.

"I just don't know, we'll see."

I was pondering the idea of owning the Audi. To have a car like that as my own, that would be pretty cool. All my buddies would be jealous. Picturing myself pulling up to the senior prom in the Audi, and especially with Neola, that would be awesome. I would feel pretty good. I was still daydreaming when Neola snapped me out of it.

"Someone's here!" she said and ran over to the monitor and turned it off.

"Hey!" my brothers said almost at the exact same time.

"Someone's here," Neola said, putting her finger over her lips to shush them.

Just then, there was a knock at the door. Neola and I looked out the front window; carefully pulling back the window's covering. It was a detective. "How did they find us?" I whispered.

"They're not here for us," Neola said.

"Oh, yeah," I said. "That was fast."

"It looks like they're here to see if there's a next of kin to let them know of Chuck's death."

"How do you know that?" I asked but then realized it was a dumb question, especially after the look she gave me. "Nevermind!" We were panicking some, or at least I was. *What were we going to do?* There was one detective at the door and one by the curb next to their car, who could see the garage and the back yard from where he stood. If we sneaked out the back, he would surely see us. "What if we just don't answer, and hide? I wonder if they will just go away."

"No, they have a warrant to search his house," Neola whispered.

"So, they're looking for evidence as to why he was killed?" I asked, already knowing the answer. "But what about the guns I planted? I thought they would throw them off for a while. Can't you just make them leave?"

"I could do that, but I have a better idea," she said and pointed to the father of the year coming out of his house.

He kicked the stroller as he passed by. It appeared he had a beer in his hand, and as he tipped it up, he saw the police across the street and quickly put it down, hiding it behind his back. He slowly backed up toward a bush and dropped the can behind it. Then he casually walked over to his car and got in. The little girl was still in the front yard playing.

"Watch this," Neola said to me and my brothers as we all stared at the man across the street. There was another knock at the door, but this time he identified himself, "This is the police, we have a warrant to search the place."

His car started up, which caused the detectives to look his way for a moment, and then back toward the house with us in it.

"He is not her dad. She calls him daddy, but he is the boyfriend of her mom. He is all she knows, though."

"Really?" I asked rhetorically.

The car's brake lights came on. Another knock at the door: "We're coming in."

The car's reverse lights came on.

The doorknob wiggled.

The man floored it and the back tires began to squeal, creating smoke. Again, the two detectives looked over at the car. It backed out of the driveway with such speed that it hit the front of the police car uncontrollably. The force threw the police car toward the detective standing near it. He dove onto the lawn to avoid getting hit. The detective standing on the porch let go of the doorknob, jumped down onto the grass, and ran toward the car with his gun drawn.

The man jammed it into drive and took off down the road with such speed and lack of control that his car bounced off the neighbor's parked vehicle sitting on the edge of the road.

"Are you all right?" the detective asked his partner, helping him off the ground.

"I think so," he said.

The two detectives jumped into their car, turned on their siren, and took off in pursuit. I was surprised the car even moved with the front-end damage it had. As the sound of the sirens faded, we saw the little girl standing in the front yard just staring down the road, looking like she was wondering what happened. Her mom came out and swept her up. As the mom turned to look down the road toward where the boyfriend sped off, we saw she had a nice shiner on her right eye. It was red and swollen pretty badly.

"Do you see her eye?" I asked Neola.

"I do. She won't have anything to do with him from now on," she said. "And I may have suggested to her that she call the cops and press charges."

"You did?" I said smiling. "I don't know if they'll have to worry about him anyway. Drinking and driving carries a minimum of five years in jail, not to mention the reckless driving, hit-and-run, and evading police."

"And resisting arrest," Neola said. I may have suggested that to him just after I recommended he gun it in reverse, hit the police car, and speed away."

"Remind me never to make you mad," I said, laughing. "Now we need to wipe off everything we may have touched and get out of here before the cops come back."

We all went to work. It became a game for my brothers. They were running around wiping everything off, seeing who could wipe the most. I'm sure the house was probably cleaner than it was when we got there. As we were cleaning, I watched Neola playing with Zach and Parker. She was running around, beating them to the things to wipe down, bumping them out of the way to grab stuff first. They would fall down laughing as they wrestled for the next item. It was amazing to see her having such fun in what was a traumatic day. She had a calm about her. It was contagious, and my brothers often experienced it with her.

We finished wiping everything we could see, whether we'd touched it or not, just in case. We left Chuck's wallet and house keys on the counter. That would throw the cops for a loop, leaving them wondering why and how they got there. We all left through the back door, climbed in the car, and drove away. Necla programmed the navigation system with the address to the warehouse. We were all quiet, thinking about what was in store for us at the river.

# CHAPTER 27

**It was a little before four o'clock in the afternoon. We** had been at the house for nearly six hours. We were a couple of hours earlier than we needed to be at the warehouse on the river. We wanted to get there early anyway to check things out, so we decided to just head there. I thought about Mom and Dad. I hoped they were all right and could hold on for a little longer. It scared me to think about what the EnGen people might have done to them. They seemed willing to do just about anything to get Neola back.

Looking over at Neola, she looked so innocent. She was staring out the window again. Even though she was around my age, there was a lot she still hadn't seen or done. I wished we could go do something to get her mind off things, let her experience life. We didn't know what was going to happen today, but if she ended up getting caught and taken back, it would suck to think about her being caged up like an animal again, not able to find out what else is out here, to see there was a normal life she could be experiencing.

"I'm a little nervous," I said, wondering what she was thinking.

"Me, too," Neola said.

"We don't have a plan. We need to figure out something!" I said matter-of-factly.

"I'm not sure yet. Maybe it would just be easier if I turn myself in to them."

"NO!" I kind of yelled but then regretted raising my voice. "That's not an option. We can do this. Besides, do you really think they will let our family walk away knowing what we do?"

"They will always search for me as long as they know I'm out there. Whoever I'm around will be in danger. I just don't know if I can live that way."

"We will end this today. We already destroyed the records in the lab. Now we just need to destroy their memories and knowledge of you."

"We'll see what happens," Neola said. "When we get there, we need to see if they have the mind blocker on. If they do, we'll need to find it and turn it off. Otherwise, we won't stand a chance."

"That's probably true. The two of us on our own with no real weapons to speak of—I see how you think it is useless. But if we put our minds together, we can think of something."

"What do you mean?" Neola asked. "You want me to try to merge our minds?"

"No, it's a saying," I said, chuckling. "It means the two of us working together to outsmart them; metaphorically speaking, two minds becoming one."

"Oh, because I thought something different," she laughed.

"You were stuck in that lab with boring scientists with no sense of humor for way too long."

"Tell me about it."

"All right, so we get there early, try to sneak in, and locate the mind blocker as you called it. Then we destroy it, and you do your mind thing on everyone. They forget and leave, and we live happily ever after," I said with a smile.

"If it would only be that easy! But you're right; we have to find that machine. I just don't think I'm strong enough to use any of my other powers yet."

"Can't you move things with your mind? Maybe you could throw rocks at them with your mind and knock them out. I remember that old Bible story of David and Goliath. That's like us going after this giant corporation."

"What story?" Neola asked.

"Oh, yeah, you probably haven't heard of that one either. Well, long story short, there was this battle years ago between two nations, and a boy had the courage to face this huge soldier named Goliath when all the other soldiers were afraid of him. The boy, named David, had only a slingshot and a few rocks to face this giant, who had a sword and armor, not to mention his size and strength. David slung the rock, hitting Goliath in the head and knocking him down. It was his faith, courage, and using his intelligence that helped him win that day. Maybe that's what we need to do."

"Arriving at your destination," the woman's voice came over car's speaker system.

Neola and I nervously looked at each other. Taking the

car out of auto mode, I pulled it behind a building a good distance away from the warehouse and shut off the power.

"Well, we're here," I said. My voice cracked a little. "You ready?"

"Sure, let's do this!" she said confidently.

"Guys, listen up," I said to Zach and Parker sitting in the back seat. "We're going to go check things out and see if we can find Mom and Dad. Do you think you two will be able to stay here in the car for a while?"

"No! We want to go with you," Parker said.

"I don't know where they are or who is out there. I really need you two to stay here."

"But," Zach started before I cut him off.

"If all four of us go walking around, they will see us. We want to be able to sneak into the area. We need to catch them by surprise. The more there are of us, the harder it will be. Do you understand? I really need you two to stay here in the car. We will be right back. So, will you stay here for me, please?"

"Sure," Zach said. I looked at Parker.

"Yes," he said.

"I mean it! The two of you need to hide here. If they find you, they may hurt you both. We don't know what they'll do, but don't expect it to be very nice. I really need you guys to stay in the car, even if it is for a couple of hours. Take a nap or something."

"OK," they said together.

"If for any reason we don't come back tonight, in the morning, get out and go find help. Walk back to the main road, find a business and go inside. Don't ask for help from anyone on this dock. They may be working for the same company who took Mom and Dad, and who want Neola. I need you two to stick together and protect each other. Be strong, guys, OK? I love you two."

"That's a long time to sit in the car, what do we do?" Parker asked.

"Like I said, take a nap, or use the car's computer to watch a movie, or get on the Internet. Just don't let the car's battery go less than one quarter left because we won't get very far when we need to leave."

"OK," Parker said.

"I'll lock the doors and roll down the windows some for you two to have enough fresh air. We will see you in a little while."

Neola waved, wiggling her fingers at them, and they waved back. I closed the door and we started to walk off. I looked back, worried about leaving them. Was that the right decision? They didn't seem too bothered and were already climbing over the seats to sit up front. Neola grabbed my hand and gently squeezed it in hers. I'm sure she knew I was worried and was trying to make me feel better. It did work some, or at least took my mind off my brothers and onto her. We continued on, still holding hands.

I parked the car a few rather large blocks away, and we walked the rest of the way. We wanted to be cautious on our way to the warehouse and not be seen but we weren't sure how easy that would be. As far as we knew, there were people hiding everywhere and they already knew we were there.

The building, which shielded my brothers in the car, was a smaller office unit. It sat in front of a larger warehouse. We walked down the front of the warehouse, between it and the building. The warehouse was an older metal building with ribbed and rusty sides. We looked in windows and up at the tops of the buildings for any sign of movement. We didn't see anything, definitely no sign of people.

Then, all of a sudden, a back door of the office building opened in front of us. We froze as I waited for someone to step out with a gun. A woman rounded the corner of the door, slightly brushing into Neola. "Pardon me," she said and smiled at us as she walked past. Both of us stood stiff for a moment, before we finally relaxed. I tried to smile back at the woman but didn't know how convincing I was. We started to walk on, and Neola stopped and turned around.

"Excuse me," Neola said to her.

"Yes," the woman said, stopping and turning around.

"I'm sorry to tell you this, but you need to call your son as soon as you can. He is going to make a decision about something today that will put him on a path he will not return from," Neola said bluntly.

"What are you talking about? Who are you?"

"I'm nobody. I just know someone is forcing your son to do something that will land him in prison. If you go talk to him now and let him know you would do anything to help him, you might be able to stop him."

"I don't know who you think you are, but my son is a good kid. He wouldn't do anything like what you're saying. Now if you'll excuse me, I have to go."

"Please believe me. Does he hang out with a kid named Danny?"

"Yes, he just met him a few weeks ago."

"Well, Danny is not a good influence and is planning to rob a store. He is trying to talk your son into going with him. Someone will be shot and the two of them will be caught. They will go to jail for a long time. There's still a chance you can save him."

"Oh, my gosh, are you for real? How do you know all this?"

"I'm not sure, I just see things. When you bumped into me, I saw your son getting arrested."

"OK, I will talk to him. Thank you," the woman said and ran off.

"Oh, man!" I said.

"I just hope she can convince him to stay away from Danny. He is not a good kid."

"You were very convincing, and I'm sure she'll do whatever it takes. We need to keep moving though."

"No mind blocker yet," Neola said.

"What's that?"

"There's no mind blocker turned on in the area."

How do you know?" I asked.

"Because I could see her thoughts."

"Well, that's good. Maybe we're here early enough to catch them before they turn it on."

We moved forward, out in the open as we walked past the corner of the office building, sneaking down the remaining front of the warehouse wall. We were about halfway across the open space when a dark car appeared in front of us, almost out of nowhere, coming from between the next two buildings. The car turned toward us and drove our direction slowly

We kept walking, trying to act normal, still holding hands. The car maintained its speed and drove past us and toward the pier's exit. We kept going but looked back every so often. The car continued out of sight.

As we came to the end of the warehouse, we carefully looked around the corner and between it and the next warehouse. Two guards were walking our direction. They didn't see us and continued walking our way as we ducked back around the corner. We could hear their boots crunching on loose gravel. We held our breath wondering if our cover was blown.

"What do you think we should do?" I asked Neola.

"Let me see if I can control them," she said. From our position around the corner, still hidden, she concentrated on the two men. "Got 'm." she said with a smile.

"So cool! I will never get sick of that," I said, grinning.

"Let's go," she said as she walked around the corner and stopped. "Come here!" she ordered the two men. She instructed them to relax as they approached us. "You will not pull your guns out for the rest of today. You don't know this yet, but you two are going to forget us but only after a few questions. Let's walk. We're going to go into this warehouse."

We walked the nearly 20 feet to the warehouse door and went in. I quietly closed the door behind us. The warehouse was empty. It reminded me of a large hangar, similar to the one where I first met Neola. There were a few large wooden boxes near the other end, and an office in the opposite corner.

"So let's see what you know," Neola continued as she looked at two guards. She stared at them but did not ask any questions. "Oh no!" she said.

"What?" I asked.

"They have orders to kill me, to kill all of us if they can't capture me safely. I don't want you or your family hurt because of me."

Before I could even respond, a shot rang out and hit the metal wall behind me. We all jumped, even the two guards. Neola and I ducked down hiding behind some large beams of the warehouse's wall structure.

"Get out of here and don't come back," Neola yelled at the two men. "Forget you saw me, and forget everything you know about me and Brad's family."

The men looked at her and then walked out the door we all came in.

"I can't see them anymore," Neola said.

"They went out the door, like you said. I can't see them either," I said, confused.

"No, their minds, I can't see their minds. I'm blocked."

Another shot rang out, this time only inches from my head. It was so loud, bouncing off the steel behind me, it made my ears ring.

"That was close," I said.

"Too close. They were shooting at you," she said as she stepped out from behind the beam. "He's behind that crate."

"No! What are you doing? Get back here! You'll get shot!" I tried to stop her but she didn't listen. She was upset and walked straight toward the large crate, probably 50 yards away. The door we'd come in opened, but nobody came in. Then something strange happened. Hundreds of small rocks, gravel from the alleyway, came floating by. They flew with great speed and hit the crate the man was hiding behind, but was ineffective.

Another shot rang out, but this time it seemed to be directed at Neola. The bullet didn't hurt her. It ricocheted off of some type of field around her. Another shot, the same thing. Neola was walking straight toward the crate, but after the last shots, she stopped.

Her hair blew up as a gust of wind blew through the warehouse. Then, all of a sudden, it stopped. A second later, the crate blew apart. It sent the man behind it flying backwards. He hit the ground and didn't move.

I stood up, amazed at what I had just witnessed. Another shot and like a chicken, I ducked back down. This time the shot came from above us, from a walkway overhead. A gust of wind blew through the warehouse, and a second later, the man flew back against the wall behind him and landed face down on the walkway he had been standing on. He too didn't move again.

Two more rapid shots deflected off whatever field Neola had created around herself. This time the shots came from the small office building in the distant back corner. Neola looked at it and then it blasted apart sending glass and wood flying everywhere.

On her left, a woman ran from behind another crate.

She ran down the wall heading toward the door. But before she could reach it, Neola sent the same wave of force toward her. The force sent her flying out through the window she was running past. She landed on the concrete outside in a hailstorm of flying glass.

I stayed back for a few seconds looking around at the destruction. Realizing it was over, I got up and stepped out from behind the beam. I walked over to Neola and put my hand on her shoulder. She jumped and turned around looking at me. She saw it was me and fell into my arms.

"It's OK," I said holding her tight as she trembled.

# CHAPTER 28

**It was quiet in the warehouse. Shards of glass and wood** covered one end of the once-tidy place. Men and women lay dead on the floor under the rubble. Neola and I were sitting on the floor facing each other. I could see in her eyes she didn't like what she did, especially hurting the guards.

"Are you OK?" I asked her holding both her hands in mine.

"No," she said. "I don't like hurting people, especially those who are just doing what they were told, working to provide for their families."

"Yeah, but some people prefer those types of jobs, no matter what. Think about it. Can you picture my dad shooting at you, or trying to kill you?"

"No."

"That's right. But these people are in this position because they're OK with doing it. They may even like it, so don't feel too bad. You did what you had to do. Do you hear me? It was the only thing you could do." I cupped her face in my hands and looked her straight in the eyes.

"You're right," she said.

"Of course I'm right. Now let's get up and continue on.

We're going to find my parents and get out of here."

"All right," she said as she got up and brushed herself off.

"Come here," I said and pulled her in for one last hug. She wasn't trembling any longer. As I started to let her go, I stopped face-to-face. Our eyes locked and I kissed her. I couldn't help myself. Her sad eyes and beautiful face drew me in. We kissed for a few seconds and then gently released.

"Now, let's go get my parents. And, well, I guess they know we're here."

We walked side by side toward what was once the small office. The door behind it was our destination.

"Did you know you could do that?" I asked.

"No, not really. I mean, it was similar to something I had done as a small child when I became angry about something, but I was never able to do it again. Besides, it was nothing like that. My toy just flew off the table. I had convinced myself I had just moved them with my mind," she replied.

"Well, it was awesome!" I said smiling at her. "Do you think you could do it again? You did get mad, and I wonder if that's the only time you can do it."

"I know how I did it now, so I should be able to do it again if I need to. I hope I don't," she shuddered.

"I know," I said as I looked down at the office building debris scattered across the floor in front of us. There were some boards splintered with sharp points sticking up and others with nails protruding out. We looked for a safe path through it. "Follow me."

Holding Neola's hand, I stepped over a wooden beam. Glass crunched beneath my feet. I let go and picked up a large piece of plywood to move it out of our way, but lying underneath it was the man who'd shot at us from the office.

We both stopped and looked down at him for a few seconds. I have been seeing too many dead people lately. I did feel somewhat sorry for him. *Did he have a family? Did he have kids?* As we stood there staring at him, his eyes popped open, startling the both of us. He was alive.

I bent down and he tried to sit up, moaning in pain. I grabbed him from behind and dragged him by his arms to what was left of the office wall. I leaned him against it. He sat there looking at us.

"Are you OK?" Neola asked him.

"No," he said. "Are you Neola?"

"Yes."

"They have your parents," he said, looking at me. "They're not here but are on their way now." He stopped talking as a wave of pain must've shot through him; he stuttered as he continued, "The... they will be in the..." he paused once again, "...the large warehouse on the end. It is the next one you will see when you step out of this door. But," another pause, "be careful. They know you're here, and more guards are on their way to us right now. You need to move."

"Thank you," Neola said, but just as she did, he dropped his head and died.

"Did you make him say those things?" I asked.

"No," she said somewhat sad.

"Come on, let's go," I said as I grabbed her hand and stood up. "We gotta get to the next warehouse before more guys get here."

She stood and came with me to the door. I opened it a small crack and peeked out. It appeared clear. "Let's go," I said and I opened the door. We stepped through. I still had her hand in mine, and I started to run. The warehouse was a good distance away, at least 100 yards. We were in wide-open space and it wasn't safe. There could have been guards anywhere, with guns pointed at us.

We made it only about 20 yards when four cars came screaming from around the warehouse behind us. Two slid to a stop beside us, while the other two stopped in front of us. Neola reacted instantly and before the guards could even get out of the two cars in front of us, she hit them with the invisible force. One at a time, the cars flipped, landing in an explosion of noise and flames.

By this time, the two cars beside us were empty and the guards were crouching behind them pointing guns at us. They started shooting, but it was of no use. Neola created the same field of protection around both of us as she turned toward them. She was determined to end this. I felt a gust of wind, and I knew they were in trouble.

Then a man and woman hiding behind the first car must have realized the sheer power Neola had, because they stopped shooting and started to run away. It was too late. The car flipped on its side and the explosion consumed them in the flames. Now on fire, they continued to run, turning toward the river's edge. The flames grew on the two of them as they ran. Just before they reached the safety of the water, each dropped to the concrete, one after the other.

Then Neola looked back at the other vehicle. Two men were already running away. With just a look, they were picked up off their feet and thrown. They hit the ground with such force, there was no doubt they weren't going to be getting up.

Neola looked around. When she didn't see anyone, she relaxed her body and collapsed to the ground, as if exhausted. I caught her just in time to slowly sit her down.

"Are you OK?" I asked.

"Yes, that just took a lot out of me."

"Just sit there a minute and catch your breath."

"No, I'm OK. We should keep going," she said as she started to get up.

Just then, a helicopter flew over and landed on the other side of the large warehouse. We could hear it was sitting there running. Neola and I got up and started toward the large building. The helicopter lifted off the ground and flew away in the direction it had come from. Neola and I watched it cut of sight, and then continued.

As we were getting close to the warehouse, two very large doors on the end facing us started to open slowly. As they did, they revealed Mom and Dad standing in the center with guards on either side of them holding guns. Then my heart sank. Standing next to them were Zach and Parker. The guards had found them.

# CHAPTER 29

**Mom was standing next to Dad, with Zach and Parker** in front of her. She had one arm around each of their shoulders holding them close. Two guards, one on each side of them, were standing slightly behind, both pointing their guns at Mom and Dad. Next to them was a nicely dressed man. Wearing a white long-sleeved shirt and dress pants, he looked like he had just come from the office. He was probably in his 40s. He had a strong face, was tall, and stood with confidence. He seemed clearly in charge.

As we approach, I could see Dad was pretty beaten up. This Frank person had really taken it out on him. I was so angry and wished there was something I could do. I could feel the rage welling up inside me. I began to tremble from the adrenalin.

"You still can't see their minds?" I asked Neola under my breath as we neared the large open doors. "No," she replied. "And the guy on the right is the head of the division. He is in charge of all of this. He makes the decisions."

"Well, we'll just convince him to let us all go."

"That's close enough," the head guy said. "Well you two sure have caused me a lot of grief," he added as he took a step toward us.

"It's the least we can do,' I said sarcastically.

"As you can see, your dad has you to thank for his current condition. Don't get me wrong, it wasn't only you; Neola contributed by not surrendering. None of this had to happen if you would have only just come back peacefully. But no! You and your new boyfriend here had to destroy my lab. Now you all must pay."

"That was an accident!" Neola yelled. "Just let them go!"

"Sorry, but you are in no position to negotiate. It is going to cost millions to rebuild. Someone must be held responsible."

"What you're doing there is wrong in so many ways," I said. "You're playing God!"

"Playing God? What we're doing is going to improve on what mankind already is. Have you seen this girl?" He asked pointing at Neola. "Of course you have! And I can guarantee there were times you wished you could do what she could, am I right?"

I didn't answer him, only stared straight ahead. He was right. There were times I wished I could. Not to take advantage of people, but to help my family have a better life, maybe even help others too.

"I knew it! So don't lecture me. I don't have to answer to you," the man said. I could see sweat starting to bead on his forehead. "This is an evil world. Terrorism is rampant; war is everywhere. This program will put an end to all of it. I just know it.

"You could've continued to study what you learned

medically to help cure people with Alzheimer's, and Lou
Gehrig's disease," I said raising my voice. "That would have
helped this world just as much!"

As I was talking, one of the guards stood close to Mom
and put his gun-up against her head. I became angry, and
scared. Neola put her hand on my arm, looked at me, and
said, "Brad." I looked at her. She had this look in her eyes.
It calmed me instantly. "It will be OK," she said.

"I don't want to lose you," I whispered to her. "But I
don't want my family hurt either."

She smiled at me. "You're sweet. I enjoyed my time with
you and your family, but it's just not going to work. We
knew that going into this."

"But..."

"Shhhh," Neola said putting her finger on my lips
before I could say any more. "Look at your family." She
placed her other hand on my cheek. "They mean more to
you than I do. And I need to get you and them out of here
safely. I will be fine. I will always remember you." She
finished and then kissed me. I lost myself in her kiss, and
for a few second, forgot about everything.

"All right, all right, break it up," the head guy
interrupted.

Neola stopped and pulled away only a few inches. "Now
you be quiet and let me take care of this," she said. I could
feel the warmth of her breath on my face. I wanted to kiss
her again, but as I moved in, she put her finger on my lips
again and stepped away.

"I will go peacefully, Mr. Roberts, no more trouble," she
said as she turned around toward the man. "But you must

let them go."

"Oh, I must? Well, I don't know if I can do that," he said nastily.

"If you don't, I will not cooperate. I will destroy anything I can and will continue to try to escape every chance I get. But if you let them go unharmed and promise to leave them alone, I will go back with you and do anything you want."

"Like I said, I don't know if I can do that. They know too much," Mr. Roberts said sarcastically.

"I will make them forget; just turn off the blocker."

"No!" I said.

"Oh shut up," Mr. Roberts said to me. "Nice try, young lady. You know I can't do that."

"Well, you'll just have to trust them to not say anything about this," Neola said looking at my family, then me. "You won't say anything, will you?"

"No," my family said almost in unison. Then she looked at me.

"You won't say anything, or try to find me, right?"

I just stared at her.

"Say it!" she demanded. "Please."

"OK, I won't say anything or try to find you," I said giving in, my heart breaking.

"There! Now let them go," Neola demanded.

"OK, I will," he sneered. "Come on. We need to prepare you for your travels," Mr. Roberts, said pulling out a syringe from his jacket pocket.

The two guards backed away slightly from my parents and lowered their guns.

"Go to your family and get out of here," Neola said to me and started toward Mr. Roberts.

My mom ran to me and gave me a big hug. The twins followed her and then Dad. We were back together again, and safe.

"Are you OK, dad?" I asked, looking at his bruised face.

"I'll live," he answered. "How are you? How did you find us?"

"I'm not hurt, and they told us to meet them here. Dad, we can't let them take her. She deserves better."

"I know, but I'll be honest, I wasn't sure we were going to make it out of this alive. These guys are ruthless, and they will do anything to protect their investment."

"But," I started.

"Brad, I'm sorry," Dad interrupted me.

"She will be fine," Mom added. "She's strong and very smart. She will do what they ask."

"That's what I'm worried about," I said looking at her as she turned to walk away. She looked back at me briefly.

Neola, Mr. Roberts, and two armed guards headed toward the other end of the warehouse.

"You, take her outside and give her this," Mr. Roberts instructed one of the guards and handed her the syringe. "We'll be along in a moment. We have to figure out how to clean up this mess. Once you give her the sedative, call the pilot back."

"Yes, sir," the woman said as she and Neola walked off.

We also started to leave. I really didn't want to go. I was torn. I felt so bad for her. I wished there was something I could do to help. I was nothing compared to these two guys with their guns. I looked back. She was almost gone. Neola and the guard neared the exit.

We were close to the big open warehouse doors. I looked back again one last time and stopped. Mr. Roberts had pulled out a pistol and was screwing on a silencer to the tip of it. He handed the gun to the other guard and I could see he said, "Kill them all; no witnesses. But be sure Neola is out of sight first."

"No!" Neola screamed. "You promised."

"Wow, you heard that from all the way over there?" Mr. Roberts yelled. "You're getting stronger and improving all those skills of yours, young lady. I can't wait to get you back to the lab. Sorry, sweetie, it has to be this way," and he nodded to the guard standing next to her. Before Neola could do anything, the guard stuck her in the neck with the syringe.

"No, stop," I yelled as Neola dropped to her knees. She was glassy eyed and appeared dizzy. She couldn't stand. The woman next to her had her by the arms and helped her sit down. Then I looked at the man with the pistol who was moving quickly toward us.

"Hurry up," Robert said. "Finish it! And you, call the pilot."

There was no place for us to go. We couldn't run. It was wide open and we were sitting ducks. Dad grabbed the boys and put them behind him. Mom stepped to one side of Dad, and I moved to the other. This was it. The man was about 25 feet from us.

I looked over at Neola one last time. It looked as though she was trying to get up. She was. She spat a clear liquid from her mouth and then stood tall. It was the drug. How she did that I might never know.

The man lifted his pistol and pointed it at us as he continued walking our way.

Neola screamed, "Stop!"

He stopped and partly lowered his pistol as he looked back at her somewhat shocked she was still awake. Realizing she might do something, he quickly turned back toward us and pointed his gun once again, this time directly at Dad. Without much hesitation, he pulled the trigger and the gun went off.

"No!" I yelled and lunged in front of Dad. The bullet struck me in the stomach and I went down. It was like slow motion. I felt a warm, excruciating pain as the bullet passed through my flesh.

"Brad!" Neola screamed and as she did, a wave of energy shot out from her on all sides as if a bomb had gone off. It moved across the warehouse but didn't knock anyone down. It just looked and felt like a gust of wind.

In the background, the generator we heard running stumbled and then died. There was an eerie silence for a moment until Neola broke it.

"Put the guns down!" she yelled and both guards dropped their weapons.

Mom dropped to her knees beside me. She began to cry as she held pressure on my stomach.

"You two leave this place and never come back," Neola ordered them. "Forget everything you know about me and this family," she cried.

Mr. Roberts was trying to sneak off. "You! Stay there

and don't move!" she ordered him and then ran to me, dropping down beside me. She, too, was crying.

# CHAPTER 30

**So now you know how I got myself into this situation.** A few days ago I met a unique and beautiful girl, fell head over heels for her, risked everything to help her, and here I am, fighting for my life. As I mentioned, everything was starting to blur.

"Hang in there, Brad. Don't leave me. You can't leave me!" Neola said.

"I want to thank you for the last couple of days," I said, squeezing her hands best I could. "I'm glad I got to know you."

"Don't talk like that!" she demanded. "You're not giving up!"

I smiled at her as best I could. I could still hear the crackling-fire remnant of the explosions and small battle that had just taken place. The warehouse was ablaze, and the flickering light from the flames shined off her eyes. Outside the hangar sat the smoldering SUV and Hummer the guards had arrived in; both destroyed. The SUV was on its side. Five lifeless bodies lay scattered around the parking lot.

Also kneeling around me was my family, all in tears as I lay dying. "You two watch out for each other, little bros," I said to my brothers. "Always be there for the other. You are two individuals, but together you can be strong."

"We will," they said in unison, tears running down their faces.

"Mom, Dad, I love you. Thank you for everything." I said. "Dad, sorry I always fought with you and never gave you a chance to make things up to me when you were around more."

"I understand, son," Dad said. "I didn't make it easy for you either. Just know we're proud of you. You sure have grown up quickly, becoming the great man I always knew you would."

"Thanks Dad," I coughed, struggling to answer. Then I closed my eyes.

"We love you, honey," Mom said, sobbing.

"You're going to make it. We'll get you help." Dad looked around for someone, anyone, but there wasn't a person in sight. Everyone had left the area the moment gunfire started.

Neola grabbed my hand, and I opened my eyes. "Neola, I'm grateful for every moment I spent with you," I wept. "I'm dying happy just to have known you."

"Stop talking like that. You're going to be fine," Neola cried.

"Neola, even you can't stop this, but it's OK. Everyone I love is now safe."

"I'm so sorry. All this power, and I can't even use it to save you... Wait, maybe I can. Maybe I can remove the bullet. Should I try?" Neola asked.

"Be my guest," I coughed. "But don't blame yourself

when it doesn't work."

Neola started to focus on the bullet. I felt it move and it hurt. I cringed in pain and cried out. She stopped.

"It's OK, Neola. There's nothing you can do," I said and put my hand onto her cheek. "I love you."

Neola cried even louder.

"Mom, Dad, please take care of her."

"We will, son," Dad said, putting his hand on my shoulder. "She is family now."

I felt sleepy. This was it. I closed my eyes.

"Brad!" Neola said, shaking me, and I opened my eyes, only briefly, to see her beautiful face once more before I closed them again. I could hear them all crying, but it sounded like they were in a tunnel. It felt like time slowed down. Now I could barely hear them, but they were still there.

Then, I felt this burning sensation where the bullet in my stomach rested. It hurt, but I was too weak to move. Then the pain stopped and I died.

# CHAPTER 31

**It was pitch black, but images were passing through my** mind. I saw my brothers, Zach and Parker. There was Mom. She looked so beautiful. Then Dad; he wasn't beaten up. Then I saw Neola. My mind revisited some of my most recent memories: meeting Neola for the first time, our time on the swing, holding hands and laughing as we left the transportation station, and our kiss before she walked over to give herself up to Mr. Roberts.

As Neola's face faded, an image of my side burning came to mind. I fought hard, but the snapshot of the bullet moving through me washed her away. The bullet wasn't going in, but coming out of me. It happened in slow motion and seemed to be going backward in time. As the bullet exited, I saw the tissue around it reversing its damage, reconnecting the fibers of my muscles and returning to normal. Then everything went black once again.

The next image my brain showed me was of my heart. The pain and pressure in my chest was so great. But it was as if I only saw it and could not feel it. As the image of my heart drew nearer and came into focus, it looked as if my heart was in someone's hands.

It was. Someone's hands were gently squeezing my heart, pumping it to move blood in and out of it. But the hand wasn't a hand. It was an image of a hand that to me was invisible.

The next thing wasn't an image. It was a loud sound, a thumping sound. *Thump! Thump! Thump! Thump!* It was a very quick and repeating sound. The thumping continued and then a gust of wind came across me. The wind blew as the thump continued.

Without realizing what it was at first, an image of a white light appeared out in front of me. It seemed to be down a long tunnel. I didn't have the sense I was moving toward the light, but it toward me. The light grew larger and larger as it came near.

Now the light seemed to be only a few feet in front of me, so bright and warm. It was so inviting. The image of light started to flicker on and off as if someone was flipping a light switch up and down. The light was glowing blue and seemed to have a flag blowing across it, blurring the light. The moving flag was yellowish and seemed tattered.

The image continued to draw closer, only inches away. It was so bright. The dancing flag was blurry, and I had to focus hard on it. Then, as if the image was talking to me, I heard a muffled voice.

The voice quickly grew louder but was hard to understand. Whose was it? It seemed so familiar, so trusting.

The voice grew louder as the image right in front of me began to clear up.

*Was I in heaven? Was this a long lost relative? No! Neola? Could it be?* Then, as if all my senses hit at once, the image collided with the sound, and there she was, looking down at me. My head was in her lap. She was still crying.

"Why are you crying?" I asked her as I reached up and wiped a tear away. "I'm still here."

"Oh, thank God," she said and bent down and hugged me.

"Brad?" Dad asked. "You're alive?"

"Hi Dad. Yes."

"Son, you died. Neola somehow saved you. She removed the bullet and healed you. She restarted your heart. It's a miracle," Dad said and smiled.

"She is the miracle. Thank you," I said, looking at her. "You did it. You just had to believe in yourself."

"You're right. I just wish I could have helped Dr. Brandt."

"You weren't ready then," I said and sat up. I felt so much better. The pain was nearly gone.

"Careful, honey," Mom said.

"I feel fine," I said as I stood up, Neola helping me. I was a little dizzy. Neola and Dad caught me as I stumbled. I regained my balance and gently pushed off of them and stood on my own. "There, see."

Looking around I noticed the helicopter not 25 yards away, shutting down its engine. That must have been the thumping I'd heard and the wind I'd felt. Then I remembered Mr. Roberts. "What about him?" I asked Neola.

"I will take care of him. Come here!" She said to Mr.

Roberts, and he walked over nervously, not sure what she was going to do to him. He was stiff-legged, and I could see he was trying to resist.

"First of all, you're a very bad person and you deserve to die. But I'm not going to do that. I'm better than you are. Right now, I want you to call your boss or whoever you report things to, and tell them I'm dead, we're all dead, destroyed in an explosion. Have your people stop searching and tracking us and my finances." She paused. "Well, what are you waiting for? Make the call."

Mr. Roberts fumbled for his cell phone, as if a scared little boy. He dialed the number and said just what Neola had instructed. He answered a few questions convincingly then hung up. He called another number and instructed the person on the other end to stop tracking Neola. That it was over. He hung up.

"Now, you'll forget we're alive. You'll remember we died in an explosion. You'll forget me as a person and only remember me as a project. You'll do your best to convince your company the research that led to my existence died with me, all destroyed. You'll try to make them do good. Make them use their money and expertise to change the research back to medical applications, to help cure neurological disorders, not genetic engineering. And one last thing, be happy and treat people kindly, as you would want them to treat you. Now go!"

# CHAPTER 32

Mr. Roberts turned toward the helicopter and raised his right hand into the air; he twirled it, indicating to the pilot to start the engine. As he walked toward the helicopter, he saw the wreckage. He stopped and looked at the cars on fire, smoking debris everywhere. The fire was beginning to spread to the hangar. He paused for a few seconds and then continued. He walked with a casual stroll, as if without a care in the world. His hands were in his pockets and he glided along, as happy as could be.

As he neared his ride, the wind from the twirling blades blew his hair wildly. He ran his fingers though his hair to put it back in place, but the wind generated by the propellers, made that useless. He kicked a small rock, once, twice, then a third time before it bounced too far to the left and out of his path to the helicopter. He continued on.

He reached the helicopter, just as he noticed something in his pocket. He pulled it out, looking at it as he opened the door with the other hand. He climbed in. It looked like a flash drive or something small like that.

# CHAPTER 33

On the dock, we all hugged each other, thankful we were alive. I was truly grateful, especially for Neola, for not only meeting and getting to know her, but also for falling in love with her.

"Thank you for everything, especially for saving my life," I said to her.

"I'm just glad I was able to," she smiled. "But you're welcome."

"How come the shot they gave you in the neck didn't knock you out?" I asked.

"I focused on it and pulled it all into my mouth. I spat it out."

"So cool!" I said. "Hey, why didn't you make Mr. Roberts change careers like you did with all the others?"

"I thought it might make it less obvious I was alive and had messed with his mind. That way, they would be less likely to look for me.

"Smart, very smart," I said.

We stood there for a few seconds looking at each other. Just as it became one of those uncomfortable silent pauses, I stepped forward and kissed her. She kissed me back, long and passionate. After what felt like a minute, but was likely only a few seconds, I felt self-conscious. Slowly stopping and pulling away, I opened my eyes and shifted my gaze from Neola to my family. They were all staring at us and smiling.

Neola and I blushed. I know I did because I felt my face warm up.

"Shall we go?" Dad asked. "Or are you two not finished?"

"We're finished," I said, smiling at Neola, whose cheeks were still red.

"We can go," she added.

I gently took Neola by the hand and walked toward Mom, Dad, and my brothers. We all headed off the pier, from where we came in. There were sirens in the distance, most likely coming our way.

For the first time in a long while, I felt like everything was going to be all right.

"Hey, Dad, wait till you see my new car," I said, smiling at Neola.

The End

# ABOUT THE AUTHOR

Steven Weaver has always had a passion for researching and telling stories. He enjoys spending time with his family exploring the great outdoors.